Imen of Atlantis
PURSUIT

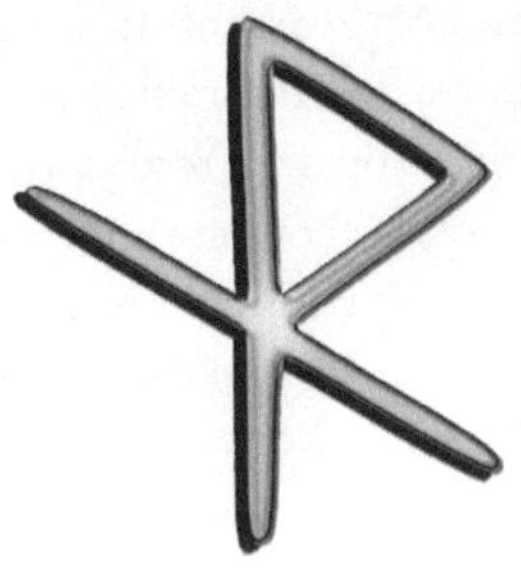

Volume Three

S.K.R.
&
TONY D'URSO

Imen of Atlantis: Pursuit

Editor: Tony D'Urso

ISBN: 979-8-89079-251-8 (paperback)
ISBN: 979-8-89079-252-5 (ebook)

Cover: Viking symbol for safe travels

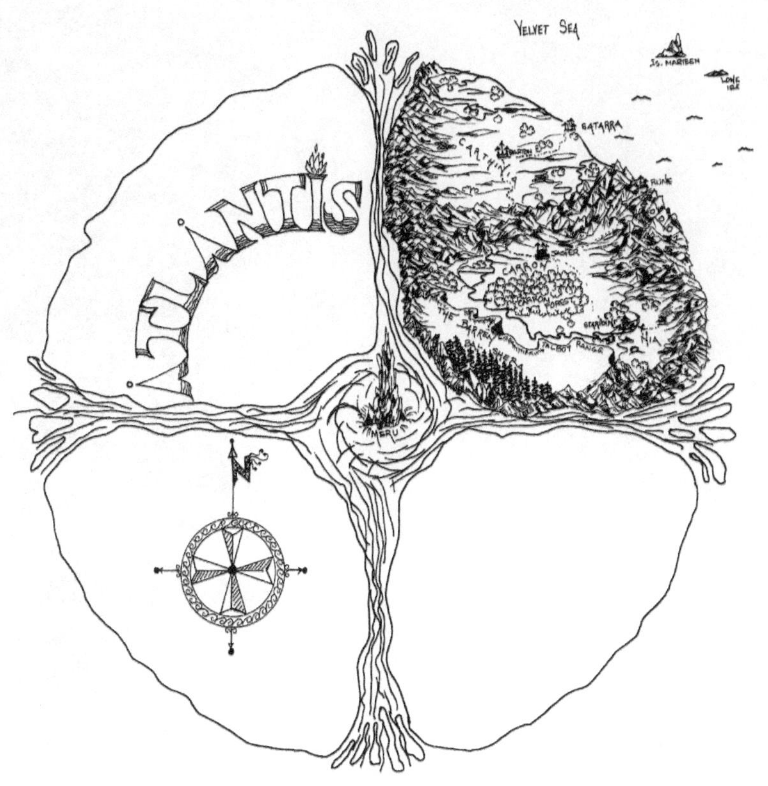

ATLANTIS
YELVET SEA
IS. MARTEEN
LONE ISLE
CAATHIA
BATARRA
RUNE
CARRON
CARRON FOREST
THE BARREN
TALBOT RANGE
HIA
MERU

PROLOGUE

BITTEN BY LUST FOR gold, the ruthless ogre Bomo hurries home after being nearly caught by Raidon and other Knights, to conjure a potion to possess Roni, using his mother's Book of Spells. *Cailloux*, the spell that will turn Roni into a pebble and back at his wish, catches his eye. But to make this, he needs the Lightning Rose – a rare flower found in the forest on a moonless night.

Meanwhile, in Imen-Hera, Roni starts feeling the repercussions of her sins—a nagging sensation within her. She visits the High Priestess and discovers there is no way back from the dangerous path she chose since meeting Eyvind. And her punishment is banishment from Imen-Hera.

Above the ground, Raidon and the Imperial Knights are going home with Laris' body when they came upon the Lightning Rose. Raidon places it on the body, and it glows. The rose's glow is later seen by Bomo, who tries to steal it but is forced to hide throughout the night, and only by sheer luck, managed to find it later when it had accidentally fallen off.

In Imen-Hera, Roni performed her last dance with Suki, knowing she will be leaving soon. She is met by her parents who painfully uncovered the truth regarding her fate. They are forced to explain their history and revealed a hidden safe region for her to live: the White Forest of Bellwin. Roni is given warrior's garb with armor and weapons to protect herself. Kenji and Suki come to bid her farewell. Everyone is heartbroken and lost.

In Jasper, Eyvind tells his parents about the Carthinians sneaking around the castle, but Audun casts his warnings aside. Eyvind also reveals Princess Adina is in love with his brother Korin, and refuses to marry her. His father divulges a few truths about the plan he has laid down for his land. Hearing this, Eyvind refuses to be a part of it and renounces the throne. This enrages his father so much that he charges him with treason and accepts his renouncement. Eyvind is no longer the Prince of Carron.

The Imperial Knights come back home with Laris' body. King Audun and his minister Aurelius come to know the whole truth about the Imen and Laris receiving the magic potion along with their encounters with Bomo. Then Audun decides that Aurelius will escort Eyvind, Raidon, and Axel into the forest in search of the Imen and Bomo.

In the other wing of the castle, Tara is plotting strategies. She sends for Adina who is told she will marry Korin instead (they found out they were lovers), because Eyvind renounced the throne.

Meanwhile, Kenji and Suki independently decided they wanted to ensure the safety of Roni and went in search of her. They found Bomo pursuing her and watched him throw a vial that bursts into shards on Roni's back transforming her into a pebble. She fell into a dry riverbed where there were hundreds of similar stones. Bomo searched the area and found a rock with red veins and surmised it to be Roni.

On the other side of the forest, minister Aurelius and his group of soldiers ordered

Eyvind, Raidon, and Axel to lead the way to Bomo. Eyvind and his men tracked in the wrong direction to fool Aurelius which caused him to show his anger toward Eyvind. Enraged, Axel charged at Aurelius, but the minister drove his sword into his chest, leaving everyone shocked. Eyvind and Raidon were devastated at this loss and knew they needed to escape.

An angry Aurelius is then about to drive his blade into Eyvind when Kenji and Suki appear, stop time, and save Eyvind while telling him about Roni's fate. The prisoners escaped under the paused time established by the Imen. Eyvind insisted to be taken to the place where Roni was turned into a pebble.

When time was restored, Aurelius found no sign nor track of his prisoners. Enraged, he decided to pursue Bomo instead.

In his home, Bomo cooked the potion to change the pebble back into Roni, but it failed to work. He realized maybe he had the wrong stone and went back to the riverbed. Eyvind and others reached the same place a little earlier and found a stone they believed to be Roni. They tracked Bomo's footsteps and went to his home to find the spell to turn her back.

Aurelius caught up with Bomo and forced him to reveal the truth. He then ordered Bomo to find the stone that was supposed to be Roni to turn her back into an Imen.

While searching the ogre's home, Eyvind and Raidon heard the gallop of horses and knew Aurelius and his soldiers were not far off. Seeing the tub of muck that Bomo had left behind, Eyvind sunk the stone into it. And it transformed back into Roni. Now the soldiers were nearly at the door. Eyvind grabbed the Book of Spells, and all three escaped using Roni's magic potion given by her mother.

Bomo is enraged to know Roni had been changed back and his mother's Book of Spells was gone. He threw a temper tantrum, and everyone was terrified. Aurelius demanded answers and was ready to drive his sword into the ogre's chest. Only Bomo's claim of being a great sorcerer and knowing many spells by heart saved his life.

In Jasper, Audun spun a tale to his Prefects about Eyvind's renouncement to the throne and his acts of treason. He is forced to reveal the real motive of this pact through the wedding of Korin with Adina. Most of them accept it when

Audun promises them great riches for their solidarity.

And so, the *Ruthless* intensify their plans of conquest and plunder of another nation in their *Pursuit* of gold and power.

PURSUIT

KING AUDUN RETURNED TO his chamber to break the news of Eyvind's renouncement of the throne to Queen Beyla. With each word he uttered, the Queen became quieter, her facial muscles tautening, and her demeanor growing almost stoic, as if she had previously perceived that something terrible was going to happen to him.

Her eyes followed the King's footsteps as he paced the room, ranting his fabricated tale of Eyvind's involvement in treachery, implicating his own son in the crime against the throne. He didn't even think twice when he stated Evyind had undermined the plans that were already set in motion by refusing to marry Adina and had plotted with his friends to overthrow Audun. He also added the tidbit about how Laris discovered that plan and refused to abide by it and was therefore killed by Eyvind.

Beyla remained expressionless in the face of such accusations. She knew her son and his principles. Eyvind was firm in his convictions and his duty toward his people and would never defy his responsibilities toward his nation or to his father for greed or power. That was why people all over the Kingdom loved him and were ready to lay down their lives for him. She refused to believe the lies that spouted from her husband's mouth. Vile were the words that accused her son of such treason. There had to be something else, so she listened and tried to read between the lines, without commenting.

The King looked toward his wife when no words were forthcoming. "I knew you would not be able to accept this fact. It's the truth, and I'm not taking any chances. After all, he's my son too. And don't think for a moment that the decision I made was an easy one. Only my father's heart knows how painful it was. But it had to be done. He'll have to face a formal tribunal as soon as Aurelius returns with him. At least we can count on Korin..." He offered his other son on a platter as a consolation.

Beyla kept staring ahead without blinking and refused to reply. She was numb with horror. This was the man she had married and fathered two sons with. A ruthless man who would sacrifice his own son to pursue his greed for riches and power.

Audun was annoyed at his powerlessness in convincing her of his lies. He became aware that unless her son confessed before her, she would not believe any of the words that came out of his mouth. Shaking his head, he pretended to be rueful of the whole situation and moved closer to her.

"All right. Have it your way. You'll hear from him soon. Directly! He'll tell you what he and his fellow Knights have been up to. I don't have to stand here and convince you of anything. I knew you'd find it hard to believe that your beloved Eyvind was capable of such a devious act. I tried to soften the blow so you're not shocked."

She maintained her silence and refused to offer a reply, her eyes focused on the wall. Audun became increasingly frustrated at her refusal to engage and his own inability to sell her his story.

"I'll need you to accompany me to meet with Camden and Tara to break this news to them. They don't need to know too many details other than Eyvind has renounced his right to the throne because he's not in full agreement with the pact. The news of his treason would shatter their trust in us. So, to save face, we can say Adina will wed Korin. Do you understand, Beyla? I *need* you there with me." Even his request was a demand.

She turned to face him, finally seeing him, and replied, "I won't be a part of your lies anymore. Imprison me in the dungeons if you must, but I refuse to implicate our son. You don't need me for this. You're quite capable of convincing others all by yourself." She took a deep breath and continued in the same vein, "Tell them I was also involved in the same treachery and therefore, imprisoned. Why do you need me now? You've never needed me in the past other than to secure Nia and give you two sons."

Audun's face turned crimson with rage. Infuriated by her boldness, he stepped forward and slapped her face hard. Beyla's neck jerked back, but she maintained her position, her hand rising automatically to clutch her cheek.

"Be warned, Beyla, your defiance won't get you far. I won't ask you again, but I'll expect you to make the right decision if you want to continue living as the Queen." His words had the ring of authority to them.

"Continue living? How can I live when my son faces execution for something he's not guilty of? You may as well send me to the gallows with him. There's no sense in my going on without him," she replied with all the strength she could muster without falling apart in despair. She didn't want to give the King any more power over her.

The King flicked his fingers nonchalantly and smirked, "His guilt will be proven soon. And need I remind you Korin is also *your* son? Just in case you had forgotten."

"He may be borne by me, but his blood is all yours. He's acquired all your qualities, Audun, and only a few of mine," she shot back.

"So, what are you trying to say? You've absolved yourself of your duties toward your other son simply because he doesn't share *your* views?"

"You're mistaken. I haven't absolved myself of any of my motherly duties. It's unfortunate Korin will make the same decisions and choices as you. He lives to please you, and if he has to banish his own mother, he will do so without any qualms just to remain in your favor. That's all," she admitted painfully, giving the King a resigned smile.

"You think that of your son? You believe he's that callous? And...and...you'd abandon your flesh and blood simply because he looks up to me? Because he chooses to strive for more and not accept the status quo for his nation? Is that so wrong?"

The King continued his rant. "How did you think we became such a powerful nation? It's certainly not by giving up our weapons and embracing archaic virtues. Korin is strong, driven, and ambitious, quite unlike your precious Eyvind, who spends his time hunting, womanizing, and charming others. Well, you can't charm a charging enemy, my dear. You have to be hardened and willing to fight to the bitter end.

"That's what sets *us* apart from the rest. Are you expecting us to lay down our arms and ask others to follow? Is this what you are suggesting? Shame on you!" he roared, not holding back his derision for her.

The Queen had nothing further to say because she knew he was wrong about Eyvind and nothing would now waver Audun away from his mission to put down her son. Eyvind was like a stranger to him. And the King had never taken the time to get to know him or understand his beliefs. Everything Audun knew was based on assumptions and hearsay, most of those fed by the evil Aurelius.

Audun, his prefects, and the Elite were slaves of their greed, their desires so voracious that even a surfeit amount would not suffice. Their appetite for wealth was hard to satiate, and each conquest increased their desire for more. They were driven by avarice and a thirst for power. Nothing would stop them now.

On the other hand, Queen Beyla was a rare and dying breed, who still held good virtues in her stead. She embodied compassion and kindness that radiated from within her. She didn't shy away from responsibilities and abided by the virtues from the days of old.

However, she too believed in fighting to protect what belonged to them and to thwart an attack by the invaders. Being a queen, she didn't shun the idea of amassing wealth but not at the cost of others or through lies, coercion, and false promises.

But her views were considered old-fashioned by Audun, and he never chose to pay heed to them, often dismissing them as weaknesses that didn't belong within the borders of Carron.

"We are a warrior race, and such frivolous, archaic beliefs are for the weak and people in the bygone era," he stated from time to time.

But this time he had gone too far and had involved her precious Eyvind in his nefarious schemes. Beyla remained stoic and firm in the face of the King's demands.

Audun too realized she was not going to fall in with his plans and come with him. He started to leave the room but hesitated momentarily in hopes she would change her mind. His eyes scanned her features, and seeing the taut expression, he knew her decision remained steadfast. He stomped out of the room, slamming the door behind him, and joined his waiting council as he made his way to the royal study where Tara and Camden were later escorted.

Audun was clever at coming up with the most perfect answers on the spot, though was not as masterful in this art as Aurelius. Still, he felt he could manage the situation fairly well, with his advisors standing at the back of the room, observing and not interfering.

Tara and Camden had their own problems to deal with after Adina's revelations, and this meeting with King Audun caught them unawares. They didn't know how much Audun knew about Adina and Korin. This meeting was important to both parties with their individual agendas.

They took their places in front of Audun in his study and waited for the King to begin. The first thing they noticed was Beyla's absence, which struck them as odd.

"Isn't the Queen joining us?" asked Camden, looking around.

"I apologize, but she's indisposed at the moment," replied Audun, faking a smile.

Both Tara and Camden found his response peculiar, considering they had seen the Queen a few hours ago, and she had looked fine then. Audun's answer worried them momentarily in case the whole plan was just a charade, and there was some trickery involved. An air of uneasiness surrounded them until Tara took up the reins of the matter and inquired about the summons.

"Your Highness, may we—?"

Before she could complete her question, Audun started speaking.

"Forgive me for the nature of this impromptu meeting. I don't mean to alarm you or make you feel perturbed, but we have an issue at hand that needs to be dealt with at the soonest. I'll cut to the chase and not waste your time. But there is some regretful news, which, if you're in agreement with, shouldn't affect our pact."

Tara's eyes widened on hearing this. Did Audun know what Adina had done? She looked at Camden and found her own fears reflecting on his face.

She swallowed hard and turned to Audun, wondering what this news could be.

"This information comes at a particularly bad time for us. However, we have the means to avert any obstacle that may surface and will follow through with our promise, despite any attempts of sabotage."

"Sabotage? What are you talking about?" exclaimed Camden as he rose from his seat.

"There's nothing to be alarmed about, Camden. As I was saying, everything is under control, and with your agreement, we can proceed forward as planned," replied Audun as he tried to quell the uproar and keep calm.

"Under control? What are you talking about and agreement to what?" snapped Tara in distress as she too rose from her seat. She was sure there was something else at play and feared the worst.

Audun realized that he was not doing anyone any favors by not telling them straight. "Let me get to the point. Eyvind has renounced his claim to the throne," he stated.

There was pin-drop silence.

Shock made its way to Tara's and Camden's faces, and they were struck speechless. Both had not expected this news and were relieved in one way because the problem *they* had harbored was now resolved. However, they wondered why Eyvind would do such a thing and if Korin was now going to be the heir to the throne. Camden looked at Tara, hoping to get his cues from her.

Tara knew she had to think fast and react in a way that would be advantageous to them, give them an upper hand, so to speak. She immediately pretended to sway on her feet and feigned an expression of horror on her face.

"What!" she screamed hysterically, wanting to get more information out of Audun. "Why would he do such a thing? Is our Adina not good enough for him? What's the meaning of this?"

In all this, she played her hand a little too far, and being as cunning as her, Audun saw through her pathetic act. He knew out of the two, she was the one who held the upper hand and who knew much more than she pretended. So, he amused her for a little while and waited for her demands before striking back. He had been using the same strategies as her for a long time—squeezing every bit of information from everyone who crossed his path.

"With all due respect, we are willing to proceed forth with this pact by offering our son Korin to wed Adina. He's the next rightful heir to the throne. We've already sent for him, and we just need your approval. Personally, the union of our children is just an added formality to the actual pact itself. Don't you agree?" he asked, now scrutinizing Tara's reaction. *Here it comes*, he thought.

"This is absurd. How can you expect us to accept something so life-changing without protest? We aren't buying cheap wares that can be switched because the one we chose has now been sold to the highest bidder," she barked out.

Audun was furious on hearing her accusing him of bait and switch. He held his tongue despite his first instinct to lash out at her. He was reminded of rumors surrounding Tara and her ironclad grip on Camden, and he was seeing it firsthand now. Having paid closer attention to her reactions, he knew she was the one who held the reins of the relationship and made all the decisions.

Thinking back to the last time he saw them, years ago when this pact was just insinuated, he couldn't recall her taking on such an aggressive stance. She had been cordial and demure at the time.

Tara was now displaying her true colors without realizing how easily Audun could read her. She was really on the offensive now. Camden saw the tilt of Audun's lips and stepped in to exert his flaccid authority.

"Surely, you have to understand this news about Eyvind is momentous and not easily palatable. First, why would he suddenly do such a thing at this time when the wedding is upon us? The timing seems to be inappropriate and gives the feel of being contrived beforehand. Second, Eyvind is not known to be impetuous," he interjected rationally.

"I know how this appears to you, but, believe me, we were made aware of this just hours ago. We're trying to come to terms with the situation and deal with it the best we can since we've just learned about it ourselves. I can't apologize enough, and the only thing we can do is to proceed as planned with the wedding and offer Korin's hand instead," replied Audun.

"And what if this Korin of yours refuses to go through with it like his brother? Then what? And what if we refuse?" Tara questioned with authority.

Her tone grated on Audun's last nerve, and this time, he refused to hold his tongue. He detested being spoken to in this manner.

"Ma'am, you're perfectly aware of the fact that Adina and Korin are lovers. I know this because she is wearing a charm given to her by him. They've been secret lovers for quite some time. So, I suggest you save yourself the agony of being affronted by this news," Audun shot back at her. They were at daggers drawn now.

Tara was speechless at the unexpected audacious comments. She became flushed with embarrassment and, for once in her life, was left tongue-tied. She couldn't counterattack his claims.

Camden broke the impasse they were in. "Audun, I implore you to use some discretion while making such profound accusations and assumptions about our daughter. We have come here on a peaceful mission and to offer our one and only child's hand in marriage to Eyvind, who you now mention has not only changed his mind, but also has renounced his right to the throne. How do you expect us to react?" He paused to take a breath and calm his emotions. "This is unacceptable, and we need better answers than what you've just offered. I feel you aren't as forthcoming as you should be."

Audun knew this was now turning into a very delicate situation, and he needed to reserve his anger for another time. Meanwhile, Tara remained silent as she tried to regain her composure. Both parties had reached a stalemate.

Audun thought hard about what to say and how to put forth his words without letting the situation explode. He needed the Carthinians for his plan, and it would be foolish to sabotage it at this stage.

"I apologize for offending you both. That was not my intention. This news has been tremendously distressing for us too, and we are still trying to process it. But as far as Adina and Korin are concerned, that's the truth. In fact, ask her about the ingot she's wearing around her wrist, and she'll tell you." He stared at Camden while uttering the next line. "Korin will soon be here. You can see for yourselves. This is partially one of the reasons Eyvind refused to take Adina as his betrothed. Now, I suggest we proceed with our plans without further ado."

"We'll have to break the news to Adina and take it from there," Camden stated quietly. He kept it simple as he was aware of the truth and tacitly agreed with Audun; however, he excused himself and Tara for a private conversation. The royal couple got up and walked to the side to confer among themselves.

Audun watched their private conversation while schooling his features to reflect calm. After minutes of back-and-forth whispers, the couple came back to the table to deliver their decision.

It was Tara who took the liberty to speak up.

"Very well. We feel it would be in the best interest of our nations to proceed with this union as agreed upon. However, because of these unforeseen changes, as you've mentioned, we'll arrange for an additional full staff to take care of Adina's needs in this sensitive time. After all, it's only reasonable." Tara's bargaining prowess was on full display, and Audun couldn't refute it even though he was extremely distressed by her suggestion. The last thing he wanted was the enemy lurking around his palace. He objected quickly and politely, "We have plenty of staff who can look after her. As a matter of fact, as many as she wants. We'd be honored to provide the handmaidens to satisfy her needs."

"It's not a matter of whether you are able to provide the necessary staff but more the matter of familiarity. It helps one from being homesick, if you know what I mean," Tara smoothly defended her position on this matter.

"Homesick? I see. She is free to visit home as many times as she needs to alleviate this. We won't discourage it. We want her to be happy," he cast off her excuse with a cunning hand.

"I appreciate—we appreciate your sensitivity toward Adina by allowing her to visit home. However, there's nothing better than having familiar faces around you, especially when one is *so* far away from home. I'm sure these things don't matter to men and don't impinge on their lives as they do on women. So, you can't possibly understand why it's so important to her," Tara explained in measured cadence.

Audun thought about it for a moment and conceded. "Women have peculiar needs these days. So, how many handmaids will she need? Four, five?"

To his surprise, rather to his shock, she replied, "At least fifty to take care of *all* her needs."

Audun was astounded at the ridiculous number. "Fifty? Isn't that a little excessive? Not even Beyla has more than five. What could she possibly need fifty for? They would only get in one another's way."

Strained laughter escaped his lips, echoed by his team of advisors. Tara didn't find it amusing or appropriate. It had a hint of mocking in it. She gave a serious but stern look that clearly indicated this was not negotiable. "Call it excessive or whatever you want, but that's the number of staff she will arrive with."

Audun realized there was no chance of discussing the topic any further, so he reluctantly agreed. He would have to have an equal number of his own staff to watch over the fifty strangers lurking about his castle. This was an unexpected kink in his plans.

Now they would have to take extra precautions with strangers staying amongst them. Knowing Tara, he expected all of them to be spies.

The meeting concluded with this, and as they parted, Tara and Camden inquired about Eyvind's fate.

"Under the law of Carron, such an act is punishable by death. Anyone who renounces the throne is a threat to the kingdom as he can later influence the will of the people and raise a revolt or, at best, divide the nation. For the safety of the state and Royal lineage, anyone who gives up the throne has to be taken down and done away with, as heartbreaking as that may be." Audun sighed and slumped his shoulders and added, "Also, in the event there is no other heir, the throne can be fought over by any challenger, and the royal lineage can easily be removed. Fortunately, in Eyvind's case, he has a brother who can assume the Royal position."

The Carthinians were not aware of every nuance of the Carronite culture, so they accepted the answers as plausible. Before they left the room, Audun informed them that due to these unforeseen events, the evening festivities would be canceled until the next day. Instead, the guests would be entertained by various supporting and acrobatic events as well as a deer hunt within a confined area just outside Jasper.

With that, the room was empty of the Carthinians, and Audun returned to his study with his advisors to seek further information about Aurelius. He needed his minister here as soon as possible to help deal with Beyla. He paced back and forth, keeping a watch for either Aurelius or Korin.

A SMALL TROOP OF AGILE horses thundered through the forest in a single file, darting around the trees and large boulders at full gallop. It wasn't until they reached a remote part of the forest, well off the beaten track, that they came to an abrupt halt.

Raidon, Roni, and Eyvind materialized from under a cloak of invisibility, startling the horses. Seeing the people in front of them, they soon settled down and resumed grazing.

"How'd you do that?" asked Eyvind.

"This potion allowed our escape, thanks to your finding it," replied Roni.

"Remarkable how a tiny drop can render one invisible," stated Raidon, still in awe at the idea of being cloaked.

"I wasn't sure if there was enough for all of us. Thankfully, there was, and I'm grateful my mother bestowed it to me," she replied with a smile.

"Why didn't you use this potion to get away from the woodcutter?" asked Eyvind.

Roni wondered about that herself. "The thought never entered my mind. It's not something I'm accustomed to doing," she replied sincerely.

"I suppose not. I'm glad you're unharmed and well," he said with a smile.

Eyvind couldn't keep his eyes off her. She was as beautiful as he remembered, even in the strange warrior-like outfit she wore. Roni too couldn't seem to escape the hypnotic quality of his gaze and shifted from one foot to the other, feeling self-conscious. The human emotion was still unknown to her for the most part.

Eyvind could see a blush rising up her neck, and realizing he was being rude, he apologized. "I didn't mean to stare…but…you look so strange in this armor. Also, those weapons are very exotic and unfamiliar to us."

Roni opened her mouth to speak but hesitated. What could she say? She felt ashamed that she needed to wear the armor and carry implements that could kill or harm another living being. She was well aware that she was now going to be subjected to the cruelty and wickedness of the new world above Imen-Hera, and she had to adapt herself to it.

It was just a matter of time before she might actually have to use the weapons. She looked down at the deadly *zoon* that hung neatly coiled at her hip and the *dandum* sticks, which were actually concealed blades. She was still half-stunned and getting used to the idea of carrying them.

Both Eyvind and Raidon saw the uncomfortable expression on her face and changed the subject. They cared too much for her and wanted her to be at ease around them.

"Your mother must've had good foresight to give you an invisibility potion," commented Eyvind.

Roni nodded her head. "It's a special potion that allows the bearer to choose how it's used."

"You mean you could've had it do something else?" Eyvind's tone reflected his complete disbelief.

"That's right." Roni remembered the loving hands of her mother, who had placed the potion around her neck, and the way her father had embraced her before leaving, and she felt forlorn. Her eyes dulled, and her shoulders sagged downward.

Her sadness spoke volumes, and both men were visibly left affected. This prompted Eyvind to want to distract her from her thoughts. He looked around and realized they still needed to figure out where they were going next and what they were going to do with the horses because it was just a matter of time before Aurelius would track them.

"We need to think about our plan of action and what to do with these horses." He pointed his finger toward them and the hoofprints they had left behind.

Raidon turned to him. "Horses are easy to track. We can't take them with us, however loyal they are to us."

"Where were you going, Roni?" asked Eyvind.

"Bellwin," she replied somberly.

"Bellwin? Where's that? Don't think I've ever heard of it."

"Not many people know about it, at least not unless you're an Imen banished from Imen-Hera." Roni had already told them about the events that had led to her leaving her beloved home.

"Do you know the way there?"

"Over the Talbot Range in the south. I'm supposed to look for the White Forest of Bellwin," replied Roni.

"White Forest?" Eyvind turned to his friend. "Ever heard of the White Forest, Raidon?"

Raidon thought hard, and somewhere in the back of his mind, there was a wisp of the memory of local lore that spoke of a White Forest a very long time ago, but never as an actual place.

"Well?" persisted Eyvind.

"I've heard of it in a tale, but I couldn't tell you where it lies."

"Do you know the way?" Eyvind asked Roni.

"I have instructions on how to get there. But as far as where it is or how long it would take to reach, I couldn't begin to tell you," she replied.

"How come we've never heard of this place?" he then asked Raidon.

"Maybe those who live there are as sacred as the Imen. After all, we still don't know where the Imen live," answered Raidon, looking pointedly at Roni, hoping she would give them a clue.

Roni understood there was no malicious intent in him, just curiosity about the unknown, and ignored his playful jibe.

Roni sighed. "I'm not an Imen anymore. I'm also no more sacred than you. I've fallen from grace. The White Forest of Bellwin is home to people like me. I too had never heard of it until it was revealed to me just moments before my banishment."

Eyvind's heart wrenched with pity on hearing this.

"I think we better leave before Aurelius gets up on our heels," suggested Raidon.

In the entire conversation, Eyvind kept stealing glances when Roni wasn't looking, still amazed to be in her presence. Roni was aware of it but didn't know how to react. She was struggling to come to grips with what she had been through in the short time she'd left Imen-Hera. Also, fear of what lay ahead consumed her. Her only consolation was having Eyvind by her side for now.

"If Bellwin lies in the south, over the Talbot Range, then it makes perfect sense why we don't know anything about it. That mountain is a barrier and impossible to negotiate," stated Raidon.

"That's true. Still, we can't afford to have them track us down, especially using these horses. Also, we have to get Roni to Bellwin without being caught. So, every move we make has to be done carefully without leaving clues for them to hunt us down," surmised Eyvind.

All their conversation was foreign to her. None of it made any sense whatsoever. She had a lot to learn about this world. She looked around and realized they were nowhere near the Talbot Mountains. Instead, they were closer to the center of the vast forest.

Eyvind and Raidon had deliberately come here because very few could get to the heart of the forest, and the paths were far less traveled than the rest of the forest. Silence descended upon them as Raidon stood deep in thought, formulating a plan, and Eyvind started pacing, wondering what would keep them safe as well as get Roni to her destination.

"First, we need to figure out what to do with these horses. They are my biggest concern. You and I can probably lead them to the edge of the forest in the direction of Jasper, while Roni stays hidden here, and then we can come back for her later," he suggested.

"No, Sire. That involves too many risks. I have a better idea. You take Roni to the Talbot Range and then on to Bellwin. I'll take care of the horses and meet up with you there," stated Raidon with unmitigated finality.

"I can't let you risk your life alone. We're in this together, and we can find a different solution to this, something that is safe for all of us," replied Eyvind with growing concern.

He knew how dangerous this entire plan was, and if Raidon got caught, he would be put to death without a doubt. Aurelius was hunting for their blood. Their chances of survival were very slim, given that they were on the run from the royal army. By now, the minister would have had every guard he could spare to scout for them.

"You have no choice, Sire. With any other plan, Roni's life is at risk. She can't remain here. This land will offer no kind of life for her. As it is, we're wasting precious time discussing this, so I suggest you both start making your way south as fast as possible, and I'll join you shortly. I promise," Raidon assured him.

Eyvind knew Raidon's plan made perfect sense; however, he was reluctant to lose another friend because the risk of getting caught was a high possibility. Both men were deep in contemplation when Roni asked Raidon, "Why do you call him Sire? I thought you were hunters."

"I'm sorry, my lady, but this is Prince Eyvind of Carron. Heir to the throne."

"Heir to the throne? You're a Prince?" she asked, looking toward Eyvind.

"I'm no longer a Prince nor heir to any throne," he replied calmly, a frown marring his forehead.

Eyvind felt very uncomfortable with having to explain it all to her, not sure if she knew how Kingdoms worked here. A bewildered expression settled on her face that begged for an explanation.

"I will explain everything to you, but we don't have much time now. We need to leave," he replied.

"I can find my own way to Bellwin. Maybe you should stay together and meet me there," suggested Roni.

She could see the melancholic air that surrounded Eyvind. She wondered what would prompt him to give up his throne and why a Prince would be hunted on his own land. Many questions raced through her head, and nothing made any sense, especially as she couldn't relate to any of it.

"Prince Eyvind will accompany you, my lady, and I'll meet up with you as soon as I can. You both need to leave *now*," Raidon stated. He rustled the horses together to get started on his own journey.

Eyvind knew that although this was a painful decision, it was the right one to ensure Roni's safe passage to her destination.

Raidon embraced Eyvind, respectfully bowed before Roni, and readied for his departure.

Both men wondered if it would be the last time they would see each other.

"You wouldn't have any more of that invisibility potion left over, would you?" Raidon asked Roni in jest as he mounted one of the horses

Roni looked at the vial hanging around her neck and held it up. A few drops were left in it, enough to help Raidon. She took it off from around her neck and tossed it to him.

"There's just enough for you. Use it as you see fit," she replied with a smile.

"I can't take this. It's yours. I wasn't serious." Raidon refused to take the gift.

"No. I'm giving it willingly. It's yours now," she replied.

Raidon regretted joking about it and felt guilty taking her gift. "But what if you need it on *your* journey?"

"I have your friend to help me. You're alone and hunted," she countered.

"I'm an Imperial Knight," he replied with laughter.

"You *were* an Imperial Knight," corrected Eyvind as he too laughed.

"Follow the white flower trail, and it will lead you to the point where you can climb up and over the Talbot cliffs, and from there, it's to the southeast somewhere. As far as I know," she instructed.

Raidon hung the vial around his neck and set off with the horses in the direction opposite to them.

"I hope he'll be safe. You think he'll find Bellwin?" she asked, turning to Eyvind.

"Raidon's been around for a very long time, and he has friends in unknown places. Believe me, he's one person who can easily find his way anywhere," Eyvind answered as he watched Raidon disappear deeper into the woods.

"The spot where you fell, is that where we're supposed to climb the Talbot Range?" asked Eyvind.

"Yes," she replied, wondering how far they were from the Range.

"Aurelius and the ogre know about that spot, and they might be waiting to ambush us. We better hurry."

Roni stood awkwardly beside Eyvind, feeling a slight discomfort at being alone with him. Strange emotions rose up in her, not being used to depending on a stranger, though she had met him a couple of times.

He could sense her uneasiness and tried to lighten the situation by joking about her fighting skills. "So, can you fight with those exotic weapons, or is it just for show?"

She laughed. "Don't worry about protecting me. I assure you I do know how to use them. I can wield them with great skill if such a moment arrives."

He was surprised by her comment because, as far as he knew, the Imen were not warring people and possessed no weapons.

How does she have them or possess the skill to wield them?

He decided to place his trust in her words and prepare for their leg of the journey. "We need to cover our tracks and make them think we stopped here for a moment and then continued on horseback. Come on, hurry!"

He broke off a small branch from a nearby tree, swept away their tracks, and covered the path with leaves and twigs to make it look as natural as possible. Roni too copied his movements until they were far enough and the forest ground wouldn't reveal their prints.

They didn't want to take any chances. They made a run toward the south in the direction of the range, moving fast, dodging the branches and tiny shrubs, without disturbing anything. On the other side of the woods, they searched the forest floor for white flowers, but none were visible.

Roni's shoulders slumped in defeat, and she pressed her lips in disappointment. She didn't know what to do.

"I think I know the spot where Kenji and Suki had taken us to search for you," Eyvind remarked.

"Is that how you found me?" Roni thought about her time imprisoned in the stone. It was a frightening experience and one she did not want to go through again. "I heard muffled tones of people's voices but couldn't make sense of them. I could not see anything other than light and shadows and no definite shapes."

"Thanks to your friends, we found you. If they hadn't come to our rescue, I wouldn't be here."

His honesty touched Roni's heart. She was surprised to learn that Kenji and Suki had risked everything to search for her, despite being warned.

They continued to moved across the forest with extreme caution, taking care to be silent but fast. Eyvind clutched the dreaded Book of Spells under his arm as they hurried along. After a while, they reached a stream to take a drink and rest up for some time.

"What do you intend to do with that book?" she asked.

Eyvind looked at it and wondered the same. "Destroy it, I suppose. It can't get into the hands of anyone."

"I agree."

"I'll have to burn it once we get to Bellwin or out of Carron. The smoke might draw attention."

Roni nodded in agreement.

"I just realized I've had nothing to eat for nearly two days," remarked Eyvind. "I'm starved. What about you? Aren't you hungry?"

"Hungry?" she asked innocently. She gently shook her head.

"I hate to admit it, but I am hungry, and a roasted slice of meat would suit me fine about now. I suppose I'll look for some wild fruits for sustenance instead and suggest you do so also. Who knows how far we have to travel before we reach Bellwin?"

Roni didn't know what to say to this and stayed silent. She sat down at the edge of the stream and looked down at her reflection in the water. She couldn't get over how strange she looked. Regret swept through her in waves as she contemplated what she had done. Thoughts of what she would be doing if she were at home flooded her mind. She missed her parents, Suki, and Kenji and was homesick. As her mind cleared, she saw the reflection of a Boad tree.

It stood majestically a few feet away from the stream. She walked up to it and touched the trunk all the way around, feeling for a passage. The tree remained sealed and didn't open for her. Her eyes welled with tears as she stroked the trunk gently. Then she remembered the Boad tree berries. She looked at the canopy above and saw a few ripe ones hanging in clusters from the branches. She reached for one branch and plucked off some berries, gathering them in a pile, and waited for Eyvind.

"Eyvind! Eyvind!" she called out softly.

He heard his name being called faintly over the draft of a breeze and rushed over, fearing for her safety.

He saw her crouched down by a large tree, and as he got closer, noticed the berries she was gathering.

"You gave me a fright. I thought something had happened to you." He sighed in relief on seeing her unharmed.

Roni pointed to the pile. "Look. Boad berries. These should sustain us until we reach Bellwin."

He looked at the berries and recalled being told never to eat them because they were poisonous. Yet, Roni was eating them one after the other. He became alarmed and thwarted them out of her hand. "These are poisonous. You can die from them."

She laughed. "Die? From eating Boad berries? Here, try one. I promise you won't die."

He was surprised at her reaction and unsure if he should eat them.

Maybe she is unharmed because she is an Imen. So he thought.

Roni looked encouragingly at him until he decided to place his faith in her hands and put a few in his mouth and bit into the fleshy part apprehensively.

To his surprise, they were flavorful—sweet and tangy. He swallowed and waited for the horrific convulsions that were a precursor to his death. But nothing happened.

"You look so surprised. Don't you trust me?" she asked.

He felt embarrassed for having doubted her. "I don't understand why they've been considered poisonous. We've been told to never eat them because they would kill us instantly. I wouldn't even let my horses eat them."

"I can't see why they would tell you something like that, especially since they hold great healing powers and are potent at satisfying hunger." She sounded perplexed at his explanation.

"That's probably why. Gives them power and control," he replied in disgust.

"They would do such a thing in your land? Lie?" There was innocence written all over her face, and he felt bad at having to break it.

"It's not a question of whether they'd do something like this but about the fact that they have actually done it and have been doing it for generations." He was quite ashamed of how people behaved here and wondered what kind of impression he was leaving Roni with about his people.

"And the people? Don't they know any better?" she asked naively.

He laughed at her innocence.

"If only you knew my world. Everyone is preoccupied with strangling one another over pieces of gold. They're given bits of gold and things as bribes for their loyalty and support. They're essentially 'bought' by my father and the Elite, and like children, they'll believe anything that's told to them."

Roni was mortified on hearing his words.

"Their senses are so dull from intoxicating greed and all the concoctions fed to them by phony healers and peddlers that they can't think past their next meal or the next gold piece that's thrown at them like scraps to a dog." He paused to take a breath. "But they're good at one thing, and that's battle. That's how we've remained a dominant force. With the promise of wealth, they'll fight and kill any enemy with a vengeance."

Roni was reminded of Imen-Hera's own ancient warring past.

"I suppose your people have no idea about the realities of such things, do they?" he asked.

"We were also once a warring and dominant race just like yours that shed blood for the sake of power and control over others until there was no other race left to conquer. It was then we were given the choice to continue at life by laying down our weapons or perish." She proceeded to tell him the historical account of the Imen and how they came to be.

Eyvind was amazed to hear it because he had never heard of such a tale.

"It must've been a long time ago," he remarked.

"Yes, it was a very, very long time ago. These garments and weapons are from that time," she replied.

Now it all made sense to him. However, he couldn't understand how she knew to wield them.

"I don't mean any disrespect, but how do you possess the skill to use those weapons?" he asked sincerely.

"Through dance. Our dances are similar to fighting routines," she replied, recalling her performances.

"Is that why you were dressed so strangely the day you saved my life?" he asked.

"Yes. I'd just finished dancing," she replied, thinking back to that momentous day. "I didn't know this was where that day would lead me."

He felt deep sorrow for her and couldn't find the appropriate words to console her other than to keep his silence.

"Let's gather as many of these to fill our pockets and continue in haste," he suggested after a few minutes.

They began to make their way south, keeping a watch for the white flower trail as they traversed the forest. The sky was beginning to lose light, and dusk was fast approaching. But their journey was just starting with people in pursuit of them.

AURELIUS BURST INTO THE study where he found the woodcutter rummaging through his possessions, searching for his Book of Spells.

"They escaped from right under our noses. You better have an explanation for this, Sorcerer!" he demanded.

Bomo ignored Aurelius and continued sifting through the piles.

"Speak, you idiot! How could they disappear before our eyes with all the horses? Unseen! What kind of sorcery is that?" he demanded.

Bomo had no idea what Aurelius was ranting about. He was busy concealing the area where his hoard lay buried. He couldn't have cared less about Aurelius.

The fact that Bomo was clearly not interested in what Aurelius had to say or even take him seriously made Aurelius furious. He picked up a jar and threw it at him.

It bounced off his back and smashed into a thousand shards. It didn't faze the ogre one bit. He turned around and looked at Aurelius in annoyance.

"They must've used one of *your* spells from *your* books!" the minister yelled out, picking up a book and throwing it at the beast.

"Huh?" replied Bomo, still dumbfounded by the whole episode.

"That Book of Spells! It must have had a spell that rendered them invisible, you fool!" he barked out at Bomo.

"Invisible? I don't remember any invisibility spells," he replied.

Immediately, he began to wonder if there *was* such a spell and if he had somehow overlooked it. *If there woz such a spell, I could've used it for me-self.*

Then he started second-guessing himself and wondered if there *was* indeed such a spell. Bomo frantically scanned the ransacked room for the book. His eyes searched wildly. The ogre poured over the entire room but the book was nowhere in sight.

He became increasingly agitated with each passing moment. The very thought of his book being stolen enraged him. He became distressed at the very thought. His muscles became taut, veins bulging out, and his fists clenched at his sides. His eyes glowed with rage, and with his mouth twisted into a mean scowl, the ogre became crazed, morphing into the beast he was.

Aurelius got frightened and stumbled backward as he clumsily tried to reach for his sword. He yelled for the guards, who deliberately ignored his cry for help for a few moments before rushing in to his aid.

They hoped the oddball *had* hurt Aurelius before rescuing him. To their disappointment, they discovered him on the floor close to the door, with the specimen across the room engaged in a violent fit. They wondered if he had thrown Aurelius clear across the room. They wished he had. The minister deserved it.

"What took you so long?" he screamed.

"We didn't hear you until just a moment ago," lied the guard.

Another guard rushed over to Bomo and drew his blade. His hand trembled slightly as he held his sword in front of him, pointing it at the ogre. It was a frightening sight.

"He's gone mad!" roared Aurelius as he steadied himself back up on his feet.

"Are you hurt, Sire?" asked the guard, feigning concern.

"No, I'm not hurt! Bring him to his senses!" he snarled at the man trying to help.

The guard hollered at Bomo to get his attention, but the ogre was in a trance, almost like he wasn't even there. They had never seen anything like it.

"Is he possessed?" asked one of the guards.

"How should I know?" Aurelius barked out.

Another guard picked up a wooden stool and threw it at him. The stool broke and splintered into pieces, but it had no effect on the crazed ogre. They were astonished that such a blow had no impact on him whatsoever.

"Is he a man or a beast?" asked one.

"He's a beast!" yelled the guard that threw the stool.

Aurelius became irritated as his men ignored him and decided to show them how to tame the ogre. He drew his sword and strode toward Bomo who, with his clenched fists and fiery golden eyes, was mumbling incoherent words. Aurelius stepped forth and jabbed the blade into Bomo's side.

The ogre felt the sharp pain, grabbed the sword with his bare hand, and yanked it away from Aurelius, who lost his footing and fell down again. Bomo looked at the sword, and in a fit of rage, he bent it and threw it across the room.

The three guards present in the room were amazed at the ogre's strength. Frightened, they began retreating towards the door.

They shouted at him, hoping to bring him to his senses "Woodcutter! Woodcutter!"

Their voices fell on deaf ears.

"Charge him, you fools!" bellowed Aurelius as he scrambled toward the door for his safety.

The three men were reluctant to do so, petrified of the ogre in his state. It wasn't until Aurelius threatened them with death if they didn't take him down that they ran toward him and jumped up on him together to force him to the ground. Dust flew all around them, causing Aurelius to take a step back.

Under the collective weight of three soldiers, Bomo was pinned to the ground, buried. The royal guards wondered if they had killed him since he was motionless. They were happy and hoped this was an end to the beast's madness.

Then, all of a sudden, Bomo erupted like a raging volcano and got to his feet, hurling the guards off him one by one across the room.

Aurelius had never seen such brute strength before. He ran toward the main door and scrambled out of the shack, screaming for more help.

The remaining two soldiers came running—Aurelius momentarily forgetting he had ordered three others to track the horses.

Out of breath and scared out of his wits, Aurelius pointed to the lair.

The men were puzzled by what had occurred, and without any questions, they hurried in with swords drawn.

Suddenly, it dawned on Aurelius that his men might wind up killing the creature if he didn't act fast and order them to take him down alive. "Don't kill him. I need him alive." Aurelius followed his soldiers into Bomo's hovel.

They rushed in to find their fellow guardsmen sprawled on the ground, knocked out. They were shocked at the sight. Bomo too stood in the middle of the room, with a bewildered look on his face and didn't appear half as wild as he had moments ago. He was no longer in a trance.

Aurelius crept in slouching, peering through the space between his soldiers until he saw that Bomo's eyes had lost the mad look. He straightened up and asked his men to stand back. He pushed forth and grabbed a blade from one of the soldiers and held it before him as he approached Bomo.

"Look here, we don't want to harm you, so why don't you just sit down over there?" he pointed to the corner, "and we'll help you look for your book."

Bomo, now back to normal, complied.

"You will? You'll 'elp me find me Book of Spells?" he asked naively.

"We most certainly will," replied Aurelius.

"That's me most prized possession. Me mother 'id it from me an' if only I'd 'ad it from the start, I wouldn't 've 'ad to work so 'ard choppin' wood all me life," he moped.

"What kind of *spells* are in this book that could have changed your life so drastically?" inquired Aurelius like a slithering snake, all ears to get to the good part.

"There're good spells in it," the ogre replied like a child who had lost his most favorite toy.

"Such as?" Aurelius continued to inquire impatiently. The suspense was killing him.

"All sorts of 'fings. Like turnin' all of you's into rats," he declared childishly.

Aurelius was furious at the juvenile sensibility of the brute. Looking at the ogre standing before him, he realized he was no sorcerer, but a mere novice at the art and a simpleton who had possessed a very valuable text that even his own mother hadn't trusted him with.

"Do you still remember the Callioux spell?"

"Course. I 'no it by 'eart. I changed her to stone." Bomo was lost in the time he had Roni in his possession.

Aurelius nodded at him. *I need this beast alive to cast another spell and capture the Imen.*

"And to reverse it?" the minister asked to assure himself.

"That's right," Bomo answered with his chest inflated, exuding confidence.

"Good. Then you'll serve as a valuable partner," Aurelius declared.

Bomo was beside himself at being declared a "valuable partner." He got off the floor and stretched out his arm to shake Aurelius' hand.

They all took one step back, not knowing what the unpredictable ogre was about to do.

Aurelius nervously held out his hand.

Bomo's gigantic hand swallowed his. It was like a small child shaking a grown man's hand. With that, Aurelius instructed a couple of his men to go back to Jasper and fetch some horses.

Meanwhile, he was going to stay behind to help search for the Book of Spells amongst the chaos, and at the very least have the ogre find an Imen and cast the spell once again since Bomo knew the spell by heart.

"You have a horse?" inquired Aurelius.

"A 'orse? For wot? A 'orse can't do the work of an ox. I 'ave an ox," he replied proudly.

"I see," replied Aurelius in disgust and disappointment and turned to his soldiers. "Make haste! And hurry back with more soldiers along with a couple of trackers, hounds, and a hawk!" he shouted.

The two soldiers dashed off into the forest in the direction of Jasper.

Aurelius, Bomo, and the rest remained behind.

"Now then, you'll lead me to an Imen, won't you? But first, do you know where they live?" Aurelius asked.

"I'm not sure, sir...but I've stumbled upon 'em in the forest 'ere and 'here," Bomo answered honestly.

"You have? But have you ever spoken to one?"

"Not exactly. I've 'eard 'em speakin' to others."

"Speaking to others! Like whom?" Aurelius asked impatiently.

"Like the blind man and the 'unters."

"What blind man? What hunters?" Aurelius became agitated at these half-answers.

"The blind man who woz in the forest but is no longer blind, but instead ee's..." he dithered.

"*He's what?*" asked Aurelius with a penetrating stare.

Bomo hesitated, cursing himself. He had opened his big mouth without thinking it through beforehand, as always.

"I *asked*, 'he's *what*?'" Aurelius was close to losing his patience with the woodcutter.

"Ee's no longer blind."

"You already said that. You said, 'Instead he's...' Well? Speak up!" he demanded.

Bomo thought hard for a plausible answer and replied, "Instead, ee's out there with me cart."

"What! Your cart? What nonsense are you uttering? You're a liar!" the minister declared.

"But, sir, ee does 'ave me cart. Ee practically stole it from me."

"What was the stature of that man?" Aurelius started pacing the room.

"Ee woz about this tall." Bomo lifted his hand to his shoulders.

"Was he stout, thin…?" Aurelius stopped mid-pace and looked at Bomo.

"Stout?"

"Fat! Was he fat or thin…his…his stature," repeated Aurelius impatiently. The creature was seriously testing his patience.

"Ee woz not stout…as u say…but ee woz very strong," Bomo lied.

"So strong that he pried the cart away from *you*?" the minister asked sarcastically, knowing the ogre was lying. "Now, why don't you save me the trouble and tell me exactly what it is you're withholding from me?" The threat was obvious in his tone.

"I'm not, sir," Bomo replied in fear.

"*But you are*, and I will have you hung for it."

"She gave eem somefing an' I'm not sure wot it woz," he divulged.

"Good. Good. What else?" encouraged Aurelius. "Look here, woodcutter, your life is in my hands, and I *will* hang you from the gallows for the murder of that Knight. Don't forget! So, fess up and tell me what you saw, and I might spare your life."

"I saw eem recently, and ee 'ad a large urn with eem an' ee practically stole me cart for the meager price ee paid for it," replied Bomo as he recalled the moment feeling cheated.

"*He* cheated *you*? And you let him get away? A mighty creature like you let him take advantage of *you*? Hard to believe!" Aurelius was yelling at him by now.

"I 'ad no choice, sir. There woz soldiers present an' thay woz questionin' eem an' I 'ad to leave. I woz afraid," Bomo admitted, looking down.

"You? Afraid? Impossible," huffed Aurelius.

"Well, I woz," Bomo replied pathetically.

"Who were these soldiers? And why were they questioning *him*?" he asked with a pointed look in the ogre's direction.

"Thay wanted to know if ee 'ad seen anyone fittin' the description of the Knight."

"The dead Knight? The one *you* killed?"

"Yes," he admitted under his breath.

"I see now. It all makes perfect sense," Aurelius said sarcastically.

Bomo was pleased to finally satisfy the man.

Meanwhile, Aurelius was furious because he was convinced Bomo was still withholding some information from him. "So what if he had an urn? Thousands of people have urns. What's so special about his? Look here, woodcutter, I'll question the soldiers who stopped you and the blind man, and if they tell me a different story, I'll first torture you and then kill you personally. *Do you understand*? Now, it would be in your best interest to tell me what was special about that urn."

Bomo faced a difficult dilemma and thought hard about Aurelius' threat. He decided that even if Aurelius got hold of the blind man, at least he still had his own hoard safe and sound.

So, he confessed to seeing a golden glint from a distance, but the man had put it all away by the time Bomo arrived by his side.

Aurelius' eyes went wild at the image of an urn full of gold. He couldn't wait to put the word out to search and turn in the blind man hauling a cart with an urn.

"I want that man found immediately!" He rushed out, screaming until he realized they couldn't get very far without horses. He kicked the ground, making the dirt dance in the air, and cursed out loud in complete frustration.

Just then, he remembered the yokel had mentioned the hunters. He turned toward Bomo. "By the way, what about these hunters you spoke of?"

"The 'unters woz in the forest."

"I know that! Did the Imen give the hunters anything?" he asked impatiently.

"Noffing."

"What? Nothing? How could that be? You're lying to me."

"She gave 'em noffing because thay asked for noffing other than 'er name."

"Her name? Of all the things they could have asked for, they asked for her name?" He laughed out in sheer frustration.

"*Yes!*"

"Who were these hunters?" Aurelius's tone changed from nervous laughter to anger.

"Some of the same ones who stopped the blind man and me-self. Thay woz Knights an' one of 'em woz the Prince 'imself."

"Of course, our beloved Eyvind and his men. Do you remember what they looked like?"

Aurelius asked, hoping the answer would be 'yes.'

"Course I do," Bomo replied with confidence.

Aurelius was stunned because it was the first time the woodcutter had said something useful.

"Then tell me everything!"

He questioned Bomo in detail about the Knights and Eyvind, and it wasn't long before he could verify it was Axel and Raidon. He was now convinced that Eyvind was telling him the truth.

"Now he's got her, and we are sitting here empty-handed, no thanks to this bumbling idiot," Aurelius mumbled to himself, pacing back and forth amidst the clutter.

"HOW MUCH LONGER BEFORE Korin gets here?" Audun asked impatiently.

"He should be here within the next hour or so, Your Highness," replied the courier.

Audun had stayed up all night in his keep, waiting for his son. Each moment that passed felt like an eternity. It was now morning, and there was still no sign of him.

"Is there no way to hasten his arrival?" he asked in annoyance.

"I'll see what I can do, Your Highness." The man bowed down and exited the room.

Audun walked around impatiently, looking out the window to see if there was any sign of Korin's approach or even the sight of Aurelius. He wondered what was taking them so long.

Time passed by, and finally, he saw a small troop of the Kingdom's horses riding hard from the north, heading for Jasper. Korin. He was here. The King watched them make their way through the gate of Jasper and gallop up to the castle.

Audun continued pacing back and forth, awaiting Korin's presence. At last, he heard the door to the room below open as Korin rushed up the stairs to his father's keep.

"Korin! What took so long?" he asked with a nervous smile. All he had to do was sell his story to his younger son and hope he wouldn't question too much.

"I came as fast as I could," Korin huffed a reply, still out of breath. The messenger who had been sent to fetch him had not divulged anything to him. "What's wrong?"

"Nothing. It just felt like an eternity, that's all," Audun replied.

"What happened? Why was I rushed here with such urgency? No one gave me any information other than that I was needed at the capital urgently. It's not the Carthinians, is it?"

"Take the weight off your feet first, son. Sit down. You must be tired."

Audun explained the details of what had occurred and the change in plans.

Korin's eyes widened, and his mouth opened up to speak, but nothing came out. Shock had rendered him speechless. "I can't believe Eyvind has abdicated the throne. So, now I have to wed Adina? No, Father, I can't do this. This is impossible." He balked at the prospect of marrying a stranger.

"Stop. Adina is the same girl you love and to whom you gifted the charm. The one you met on that island."

"What? She's a Princess?" Korin was embarrassed to have his truth come out before the King, but he was equally shocked and delighted to know she too was royalty.

"What a coincidence! How awkward it would have been if Eyvind had married the woman I love."

"What about Eyvind, Father?"

"Eyvind is a fool. He refused to be a part of our plans and didn't want to marry Adina once he saw the charm around her wrist."

Korin wasn't surprised by his brother's actions. Eyvind lived by his own principles and most often, they were totally opposite to the King's and his plans. "What will happen to him now?"

"I am saddened to say this, Korin. But the only way to prevent a revolution and stop people from joining in the uprising in support of your brother is to have a 'trial' and find Eyvind and his cohorts guilty of treason and hang them to quell a foreseeable rebellion. We want our plans to run smoothly now and in the future." Audun looked at his son's face to gauge what he was feeling.

The original plan was to have Eyvind wed Adina and, in the process, increase their camaraderie with the Carthinians. Then Audun planned to bait the Carthinians by inviting them to engage in a joint expedition with the Carronites and invade Bodon stealthily to claim the gold stolen from an armada that had capsized on its shores. They would have shown them the report given by the survivor, who had managed to make his escape through the deadly caves of Bodon and land into Korin's wicked hands.

They would allow the Carthinians to head the expedition into Bodon and supply them with a map that would bring inevitable casualties as a result of ambush. They estimated the Carthinians would keep sending more troops to engage the Bodonians. When the time was right, the Carronites would enter through back tunnels and wipe out both.

Simultaneously, they would order an attack on Carthinia and manage to defeat them. Having defeated Bodon and capturing the hidden wealth, along with taking over Carthinia, Carron would stand undefeated.

Nobody would know about the actual riches that lay in the form of vast gold veins marbling the mountains of Bodon. The gold ore would be extracted by a special, hand-chosen group of miners led by Audun's loyal supporters.

Carron would then declare supremacy over all the lands and share the spoils with the prefects except for the gold ore. That would remain in the hidden coffers known only to Audun. The Carthinians remained as their only obstacle until now.

But with Eyvind defecting and Beyla not cooperating, the new turn of events threatened to upend this plan, forcing Audun to entertain the thought of disclosing the existence of gold ore in Bodon in order to sweeten the deal and ensure compliance. Also, there was a group of prefects who remained loyal to Eyvind and would never believe the story of treason. To sway them over to his side and gain their fidelity, Audun would have to give them more than just the spoils of war.

"We need these prefects along with their lieges, including the common people, for support. We can't have half-hearted promises or commitments," Audun stated in distress. "I've not told them of the ore. So far, they've only been promised a share in Carthinia's plunder. You know there are some who'll ultimately refuse to comply in protest because they have pledged silent allegiance to your brother. Then there's a possibility the Carthinians might balk at the idea of heading an invasion into Bodon. They're already suspicious of us."

Korin listened quietly as he digested the new dilemma.

"We'll have to wait longer to execute our plan and by then, Eyvind would have faded from the memories of his loyalists, and the Carthinians would have lowered their guard."

Korin kept his expression blank and did not react to his father's declarations.

That worried Audun. *Is he also having a change of heart?*

He placed a hand on Korin's shoulder to remind him of the plans made long ago. "All our hard work is finally coming to fruition. By a strange twist of fate, you will even get to wed the woman you love. How much better can it get?"

Korin nodded in agreement but without much enthusiasm. In a matter of days, since his absence, things had changed drastically, and all their plans to keep the gold ore in their personal treasury were lost to them.

He was sunk deep in thought as he wondered how much more they would have to give up in return for loyalty. He couldn't believe the turn of events that had occurred with just one decision taken by Eyvind. He shook his head to clear the thoughts and knew they had to deal with what they now faced.

Meanwhile, looking at Korin's silence and stoic mien, Audun was concerned. He couldn't have another one of his sons rebelling against the change of plans. "You're not changing your mind, are you?"

Korin snapped back into reality. They needed to make some practical decisions now. "How much are you willing to relinquish to these prefects in return for their support, father?"

Both of them discussed the strategies to execute the plan and distribute the spoils. They recoiled at the idea of giving up a significant portion of their plunder.

Korin suggested, "Father, I don't think we should distribute everything equally amongst the prefects, just give them enough to be happy and loyal. The rest should stay with us. Also, make me in charge of mining Bodon's gold so the true amount can be hid. This allows complete control of the wealth, and we dole it out as needed."

"Excellent Korin, it'll ensure our complete control over everything. But it's annoying that we cannot take action at once. This'll only add more time to a plan that's already lengthy. I suppose we have little choice left now."

They discussed the minor details, and then the King asked Korin to rest.

As he was about to leave, a thought struck him. "What about Mother? How'd she take Eyvind's news?"

Audun lowered his head and gave it a rueful shake. "She chose the same fate as him."

Korin was shocked that his mother would choose to forsake him and his father. He knew she had old-fashioned principles just like Eyvind, but he always thought she had loved both her sons equally. *I suppose not. Eyvind has always been her favorite.*

"I see." He nodded once, staring off into nowhere, then got up to leave.

"He's her favored son, after all," he muttered under his breath as he made his exit down the stairs.

"Don't forget about tonight," Audun shouted out after him.

Korin raised his hand in acknowledgment and disappeared down the steps.

Audun paced the room, processing everything that had transpired in the past two days, wondering what he was going to do about Beyla. She was well-liked and popular amongst his people, and he had to be cautious and diplomatic about his actions. Though he had severed his relationship with her without compunction, he was aware he couldn't reveal the same in public.

He formulated several plans on how to deal with her, but most were unworkable. When it came to masterful lies, Aurelius was the authority. Thus, he left the task to Aurelius to come up with a convincing plan.

This decision brought him relief, and with that, he too vacated his chamber in the high keep.

IT WAS LATE FALL, and winter was just around the corner, waiting to lay down its frigid grip upon the lands. The brisk breeze and frosty chill indicated it was just a matter of weeks or even days before the lands were covered with a thick blanket of snow.

Tara looked out the window of their chamber, deep in thought, and cracked it open to feel the breeze. It was icy. She quickly closed it and began pacing the room. It was obvious something was churning in her conniving mind; however, this time, it was fear that brewed.

She turned to her husband. "Do you realize winter is just days away? I don't trust them. They're deliberately stalling us. They want us to get stuck here, and when the winter comes down hard on the land, they would ambush us on our way back. I just know it. We need to leave immediately."

"Why must you always be suspicious of everyone?" he asked.

Tara was furious at Camden's laid-back approach and growled out her answer.

"Because my suspicions have served us well. That's why!"

On any other day, Camden would have chosen to stay silent because most times, it was futile arguing with her. However, not today. "We both came here to accomplish a task, and yes, I know they've changed things on us, but you and I both know the switch has worked in favor of Adina. Can you imagine what would have happened to her if Eyvind hadn't stepped down? How awkward that would have been for her."

He raised a hand in front of her before she could interrupt him. "It's the best thing for us. Besides, we get to install more spies in this situation than we would've otherwise. It is serving as a fortuitous bargaining chip, if I may say so. I suggest we put aside our anxieties and suspicions and move through with this. Also, if we tried to leave now, don't you think it might make *them* suspicious? What if that compels *them* to attack us for refusing to go through with it?"

"Are you implying we should go through with this out of fear of retribution? What kind of people do you think we are? Have you no pride in yourself? You should be ashamed of yourself!" she spurted in a fit of rage.

"Control yourself, Tara. I'm just stating the reality. Adina's affair with Korin has been beneficial in more than one way. We've gained an advantage we didn't have before. And as far as being cowards, I'm *not* a coward, but we are deep in enemy territory. And yes, we have some soldiers with us but not enough to fight off all their forces. They can wipe us out in one swoop, not to mention, then take over Carthinia easily once we are gone. Did you ever think about that before you made the irrational decision to leave abruptly?"

Tara was not used to her husband speaking to her so plainly. "I'm no fool, Camden, and I resent your insinuations. Don't forget you wouldn't be where you are without my talent and brilliance."

She used her words to castrate her husband yet keep him in her control. Camden knew this and had become numb to her emasculating jabs. She had reduced him to the level of a puppet, where he did as he was told without question, most of the time.

But not this time. He was not going to let her make the decision for them because he understood diplomacy and conflict much better than she. And he loved their daughter more than her. "I won't allow you to make an impulsive decision. That's final! We've worked hard for this for many years, and here we are—inside the impenetrable walls of Jasper."

He continued further, "Do you know how many of our ancestors lost their lives trying to get close to these walls, let alone enter the fortress city? The cliffs are red not just because of the stone but because of the blood spilled by our ancestors, trying to reach these gates. And here we are safely ensconced within the walls of this wretched city without having spilled a single drop of blood."

Finally, he added, "On this matter, I have to disagree with you and put my foot down and insist that we stick to our original plan and arouse no further attention or suspicion."

Tara knew there were some things her powers of influence could not reach, and this was one of them. Although she knew he was right, she refused to back down without having the last word.

"All right, Camden. Go ahead with your plan, but may I remind you that if I sense a single hair out of place, I'll take the first opportunity to head home as fast as the wind will carry me… with or without you. I won't stand by and be taken prisoner."

Camden allowed her to have the last word and remained silent.

Tara walked out of the chamber and had the chambermaid fetch Adina.

Camden feared the verbal assault she was going to unleash upon his daughter. Tara always managed to take her defeat out on someone in the end.

It wasn't long before Adina entered their chamber looking very frightened, and when she saw the state of mind her mother was in, she feared the worst, wondering what had transpired since she last spoke to them.

Camden saw the fear and uncertainty on Adina's face and helped ease the tension by taking her hand and walking her to a settee. "How's my darling?"

Adina's gaze remained transfixed on her mother. Fear was emanating from her in waves.

Tara was pacing the floor with her hands clasped together behind her and her head bowed low. It was hard to guess what haunted her wicked mind.

Camden sat down beside his daughter and gently squeezed her hand.

Having feared the worst, Adina couldn't stand the suspense any longer. "What happened?" she asked her father softly.

"Your mother and I met with Audun earlier," Camden began.

Adina forced herself to turn away from her mother and look at her father briefly. She was terrified to find out the outcome and remained silent as he imparted the news.

"You'll wed Korin. Lucky for you," Tara stated sternly like an evil witch.

Adina was shocked to hear the news. She wondered what happened to Eyvind and how this came to be. She was perplexed by the whole thing. After all, Eyvind was the heir to the throne and not Korin.

"What about Eyvind? He's the heir to the—" She was interrupted by her mother.

"He's no longer the heir, so you don't need to worry your silly little head over it," she blurted with annoyance as she continued to pace the floor.

Adina couldn't understand why her mother was so annoyed and wondered what else had transpired that had her on edge. She was overjoyed with the news but was unable to show relief because she was bothered by the rage that was brewing in her mother's eyes.

She carefully posed the question, trying not to set her off in any way. "So—I don't understand. Is there more to this? You look distressed." She looked at her father and then back at her mother, who continued to pace without making eye contact with her daughter.

"Father?" she asked, hoping he would reveal something to her. Meanwhile, her elation was drowned by terror and anxiety about what was troubling her mother so intensely.

"You *are* still in agreement to marry Korin, aren't you?" he asked gently.

"Yes. Of course, I am!" she replied without hesitation. She was even more confused by his question.

"Well, you better be! You've caused enough strife as it is," Tara interjected angrily.

Adina was rueful of her actions but unaware of why this caused her mother such consternation, especially since Eyvind had stepped aside to allow his brother to marry her. Then it suddenly occurred to her to inquire about why Eyvind had relinquished his right to the throne.

"Did Eyvind willfully relinquish his position, or was it forcefully pried from him?" she asked with deep concern.

"How does it matter to you? You have what you wanted, don't you?" she shot back.

Adina resented being talked to like an incompetent child by her mother. No matter what she did, she was unable to please her.

"It's not that I don't *have* what I *want*. It's just that I care about how Eyvind was removed. It makes a big difference if he did it of his own volition or if he was forced out," she retorted.

"Still not satisfied! That's your daughter, Camden!" Tara snapped at her husband.

"What do you mean by that, Mother? It's not an unreasonable question. Why can't I get a simple answer?" Adina asked with suppressed anger.

"Like I said, what difference does it make now? You have what you wanted," replied Tara, relishing the power of control over her daughter and Camden.

"Well, it does to me. It's an honorable thing if he did it of his own volition. Then again, what would you know about honor?" she lashed out unrestrained for once.

Adina could hardly believe the words that were pouring out of her mouth. She couldn't believe she had finally stood up to her mother. She was pleased with herself but at the same time, very frightened. Tara was not to be messed around with.

Her statement shocked her parents. Adina had never dared to raise her voice or speak back to her mother, ever.

Tara could not believe Adina's audacity. She raced over to slap her face, but her hand was pulled back by Camden before it could make contact with Adina's tender cheek.

"Stop it! I won't allow this mindless repression of simple information. She deserves an answer," he exclaimed in anger.

"Let go of my wrist!" Tara shouted, pulling away her arm. "She created this mess, and she can find out the answers from her lover." She looked at Adina with contempt.

Adina could not figure out why her mother was so enraged, but then again, it never took much to set her off, especially if things didn't go according to her plan.

Camden decided it was best if he stepped in to explain things to her. He told her everything that had transpired, and Adina's eyes filled with tears. She became overwhelmed with emotionwhen told Eyvind had relinquished his right to the throne of his own volition.

She was impressed with his sense of decency and chivalry. Adina was a hopeless romantic and was touched deeply by such gestures. Camden withheld Eyvind's fate from Adina for now.

Tara stood by the window with her arms crossed tightly in front of her and stared out. She was disgusted by her daughter's emotional response and her obsession with romance. She stewed as she listened to the conversation happening in the room behind her back.

In Tara's eyes, her daughter had displayed the ultimate sign of weakness, and it was the one characteristic she loathed. It was difficult for

Tara to accept her as her own flesh and blood. Often, she wished she had borne a son instead. Her daughter could only possess weaknesses inherited from her father.

Tara examined Camden's shortcomings and was sickened by them. *Why can't he be more aggressive and heavy-handed in dealing with such matters?* She was frustrated and discontent with her life. She wanted more.

Tara looked around the room to take in the opulence, elegance, luxury, and rich culture the Carronites possessed. She walked up to the curtains and felt the plush fabric between her fingers. The detail and indulgence of the fabric were a stark reminder of how primitive the Carthinians appeared in comparison. They were a seafaring nation with little resources and lacked the sophistication of the Carronites.

That made her seethe with jealousy. Her frustrations with her husband and daughter only added fuel to the fire. Tara coveted everything the Carronites possessed and wanted it for herself at any cost.

She began to imagine herself as the ruler and Queen of Carron. Her ambition grew and secretly took root. She was determined she would fulfill this goal one way or another, with or without Camden.

Meanwhile, Adina remained speechless and wept silently. They were tears of joy mixed in with those of sadness for Eyvind. But it wasn't long before she was struck by the petty thought of what she was going to wear to the formal introduction to Korin that evening.

She got up abruptly, wiped the tears from her face, and excused herself as she dashed off to get ready.

KORIN USED THE SECRET passageways to make his way to his mother's chamber. As he entered the hidden door, he heard soft murmurs reverberating in an almost silent room. From the threshold, he could see it was coming from the southeast-facing windows.

There, he found his mother clad in traditional white mourning robes, sitting on a low tufted seat and softly humming an ancient hymn from Nia. In a meditative pose with an air of isolation enfolding her like a cold mist, she looked like a condemned prisoner awaiting her sentence. Her fretting chambermaids could only keep watch over her but do nothing to alleviate her pain.

Korin observed all this for a couple of minutes and then decided to approach her. The chambermaids gave way until he was standing next to his mother, hoping she'd acknowledge him. But she was in a world separate from his as she continued to stare forward and keep whispering the ancient hymn. He wanted to say something.

What do I say? What can I say? She has made her choices.

He was caught in a conundrum. On one hand, he faced losing his mother forever, given the decision his father was making, and on the other, all his hard work thus far would be sacrificed if he chose his mother. He couldn't let go of the prospect of obtaining the vast amount of fortune awaiting him. He briefly struggled with his conscience; however, in the end, his avarice for wealth and power won him over.

Beyla continued to chant her hymn without pausing, while Korin walked around and stood before her. She was aware of his inner struggle and allowed him to come to his own conclusion. She knew her son well and was certain of his decision. Yet, there was a tiny sliver of hope that yearned for a different outcome.

Words danced on the tip of Korin's tongue but never escaped his lips. He hesitated, then opened his mouth to say something, but his greed blinded him. He fought hard against the urgeand suppressed the words deep within him.

The fragile thread connecting him to his mother, right from the womb, urged him to sway her from her decision. But his instincts knew she made up her mind, and it would be futile to change it. There, at that moment, he was completely powerless.

His love for his mother died a slow death as his raging ambitions took over him like intoxicating demons, steering him away from making a rational choice. In the end, his demons succeeded as he abruptly turned around and walked away without uttering a single word.

He traversed the room, and the door closed behind him. Just before it was sealed shut, he turned to take one last glance to check if his mother had broken her meditative state to look in his direction. She hadn't.

Korin felt a deep tear within him, but he reminded himself of his duty to his nation and the task he had committed to. He was not about to abandon what had taken him and his father years to formulate.

Wearing a mask of cold indifference, he made his way to his chamber to prepare for the evening festivities, but not before summoning the royal Healer, Derrik. A man devoid of scruples like the rest, he was neither a healer nor a royal, just Aurelius' cousin, who had risen to power, thanks to the minister, sharing his similar lack of values. Both were conniving, calculating, and power-hungry. His talents lay in concocting tonics that numbed the mind or suppressed the conscience.

Korin needed something to numb him for the task he was about to undertake. Waiting for the Healer in his room, he thought about Adina. His feelings for her had changed immediately upon the discovery of her identity. The thrill of the chase of a forbidden relationship had vanished. It was both the mystery and secrecy of their meetings that had drawn him to her. He had never intended to discover her true identity or pursue marriage with her.

Hearing the King's words, he lost the yearning to see her, as there was no treading of dangerous territory to rendezvous with her. The relationship had lost its exotism, now that he was bound into marriage, with no way out. A soft knock on the door brought him out of his reverie as his varlet led Derrik in.

Derrik was surprised to see Korin requiring his services and not the King since Korin was known to be away from the palace most of the time. Also, the Healer was not aware of the recent events that had unfolded within its walls.

"Highness, I didn't know you were back. When did you arrive?" he asked Korin, moving hurriedly in his direction, with his hands clasped in front of him. The short, stout man was adept at displaying insincere concern for others, especially the royal family.

The Healer was dressed in his royal regalia—a long black robe edged with a gold border and a dark pillbox hat that had golden sides. He came to a stop in front of the young Prince and bowed low.

Korin seemed preoccupied, a frown making tracks on his forehead. "I didn't expect to be here either," he mumbled under his breath.

If there was one thing that Derrik was proficient in, it was the art of reading people with a fair amount of accuracy. He could tell by the perturbed look and dark tone that something serious had occurred. He waited for the Prince to speak up.

"Healer, get me the strongest tonic that would completely numb a person from the inside out and suppress compassion or even pity and another one that would lead to a lethal outcome. Make sure no one knows about this."

Derrik was taken aback at this highly irregular request but kept his expression blank. He knew better than to ask questions. Losing his tongue was not something he looked forward to. Korin's request translated into something sinister that was about to take place. Derrik salivated at the opportunity of dispensing such potions because it always promised the occurrence of a malicious event or two. He lived for moments like this where he could be in the center of things. His suspicions were strongly on the foreign guests. The Carthinians were Carron's main targets.

Little did he know that even his wildest guesses couldn't have landed him on the actual reason why Korin sought these concoctions at this time.

"Pardon my impertinence, Your Highness, but what's the nature of the demon that requires this rare request?" Derik tried to be inobtrusive in his question, thinking himself to be clever, but it landed in the wrong way.

Korin's eyes darkened, almost becoming black, as his muscles tensed in rage at the Healer's intrusion.

Derik took a step back and cast his gaze to the ground, picking up on the Prince's emotions, then respectfully nodded in agreement and set off to prepare the potions.

Before he left the room completely, Korin stopped him and asked, "How long will it take? I need them right away."

"I'll get started on them immediately, Sire. Shouldn't take me more than half a day or so for the lethal mixture."

"Not good enough. You'll have to do better than that. I need them within the next two hours," Korin ordered.

Derrik was perturbed by such an impossible demand, but he didn't dare to argue with the Prince. He was aware Korin would not hesitate to have him disappear and install another Healer in his stead. However, he also didn't want to fail in this order and not deliver. He was caught in a quandary and tried to put forth his point. "Your Highness, it'll take me time to gather the necessary ingredients—"

But he was rudely interrupted. "Two hours, Derrik! Or you can use that potion on yourself," Korin blasted.

Fear ran through him, and for the first time, Derik trembled. He was now facing a difficult task and had no choice but to comply. "Ve-very well, your highness. I-I'll do my best," he managed to stutter.

He was shown to the door by the varlet and seen out.

Once Korin was alone, he stared out of the window for a long time, trying to calm his raging thoughts. His servants knew better than to disturb him when he was in this mood. When the sun was close to setting, the Prince turned around and grabbed the festive clothes laid down for him and changed into them, giving his approaching varlet a look that would have skewered him on the spot. The man halted and walked backward to his place in the shadows from where he could unobtrusively wait for his orders. This was not the day when Korin wanted people around him, yet he knew he had to prepare himself to be cordial and affable during his formal introduction to Adina.

Before he left the room, the Prince snapped his fingers in the air, and the varlet quickly fetched an ornate glass bottle, his fingers trembling as he poured the contents into a goblet. The Prince snatched the goblet from the man, and tilting his head back, he threw the contents down his throat, the warmth of the brandy making its way to his gut and into his blood. This helped his anger settle down a notch.

He then patted his pockets, looking for something, and immediately his varlet produced it. A small metal flask that Korin seized from him and discreetly tucked away in his pocket. He then walked out of the room, and the varlet heaved a sigh of relief, having survived the tempestuous mood the young Prince was in.

The evening festivities were soon to begin, and the guests had started gathering in the grand hall. Audun paced in his study, desperately trying to think of a plausible reason for Beyla's absence. He was consumed with worry, wondering if people would believe his excuse. He wished Aurelius were here to ease his burden.

This was not the time for errors. After all, the Carthinians were on high alert. Tara would be closely observing everything today. She was the one who truly troubled Audun. The woman was suspicious of everyone and distrustful of everything.

Moments ticked by fast, drawing closer to the time when the formal festivities were to begin. Audun waited until the last minute to leave his study, and just as he was about to depart, Korin appeared at the door of the secret passageway.

"I am glad you're still here," he whispered to his father.

"Is everything all right?" Audun was surprised and confused to see him. "I thought you would be at the gathering hall."

"I thought I might accompany you," replied Korin, his voice clipped.

Audun felt a sense of comfort at having him by his side to detract him from his own nervousness, but he knew his son well. Korin might appear calm and collected, but the stormy eyes told him a different story. Audun knew he was up to something. But what?

Do I really want to know what he has done? The King was not sure he wanted the answer to his thoughts. He felt a strange sick feeling in his gut that rose up his throat, choking his thoughts. He forced himself to swallow the emotions, not wanting to know its source. Yet he had to make certain his mind was not playing tricks on him, given that he had been under severe stress, had little sleep, and was not thinking straight.

He opened his mouth to ask Korin, but his question was not allowed to be given voice.

"It's all been taken care of, Father. Let's get this evening over with."

Audun did not want to probe any further or know what his son had done but was confident he wouldn't betray him like Eyvind had. He trusted Korin explicitly and implicitly and was confident things were under control.

Both men went to the gathering hall and made their grand entrances.

Korin caught sight of Adina, who stood by her mother. She looked ravishing in her pale rose gown like a flower about to blossom. Her blushing cheeks told him she was aware of his admiring glances. He waited for the introductions.

Adina was indeed elated to see him but contained her glee with great difficulty behind her ornate fan (Tara didn't want her daughter to display her emotions in public). There was always a royal façade to be maintained. Adina settled with sneaking Korin a smile when no one was looking.

Korin turned his cold eyes away from her and did not reciprocate. Being the Prince, he could not openly show his feelings, but he too found himself feeling joy and excitement when she smiled at him, something he had least expected.

Adina was hurt and confused by his reaction but dismissed it.

What were you expecting? We are at the royal hall, and introductions are yet to be made. Of course, he is not going to smile at you. You're being silly.

She knew the Carronites would have a different set of royal behaviors that Korin would have to follow. She gave a tiny shake of her head to cast out all doubts and stepped forward.

His father introduced Korin first to Camden and Tara, who smiled graciously but with covert displeasure.

Tara looked around and noticed Beyla was once again not in attendance. "Where's Beyla? Is she still *indisposed*?" she asked with growing sarcasm.

Korin was quick to answer, "She's not well. The Healer has requested she get as much rest as she can. She has succumbed to a sudden illness that is puzzling us all."

"Is *that* so?" There was an overt tone of disbelief in her voice.

Korin found Tara insufferable and detested her insinuation.

"That *is* so," he answered with a finality, daring her to argue.

Tara shot a glance at Audun to catch his reaction, but he remained stoic. She wanted to believe them, but their answers did not sit right with her.

"Odd. Very odd that someone could be overcome by such a devastating illness overnight," she commented.

"She didn't quite succumb to it overnight, Your Highness. She's been battling it for a while, and the tension of this whole affair has put her under," Korin retorted in complete confidence.

Although she couldn't detect a quiver in his voice, indicating he was lying, she remained unconvinced. She decided to throw another stone at the calm front the duo presented. "I'd like to pay her a visit this evening. Must be terrible to be cooped up in her room, dealing with such terrible news all alone. Meanwhile, others are enjoying the festivities, and the poor creature is all alone. I'm sure she could use some company," she replied, reeking of insincerity. And with that, she pushed through the crowd and made her way to be seated at the grand table.

Korin was left speechless. He had to find a reason to excuse himself and see the Healer before Tara paid a visit to Beyla. Korin beckoned one of the waiting staff to deliver a message to Derrik. He scribbled instructions on a piece of paper and handed it to him.

All of them moved to sit down to dine, and Adina was seated next to Korin. His fingers crept under the table to find hers, and he held her hand, throughout dinner, making her glow in happiness. She made small talk while eating and expressed her awe about how fate had brought them together forever.

Korin nodded, but remained cold and distant, not contributing much to the conversation around him.

She began to worry and wanted to be reassured that everything was fine between them and this was what he too wanted. She whispered, "Is something the matter, Korin? You don't seem to be glad to see me. Are you disappointed?"

He became annoyed by her questioning but withheld his irritation. He schooled his expression to appear worried and explained. "I'm sorry, Adina. I'm just worried about my mother. She's very ill."

Adina felt guilty for seeking attention under such circumstances.

"Why don't we visit her? It'll settle your mind and put you at ease," she suggested in eagerness to show her support.

Korin was caught off guard by her suggestion. *No, not this one too. What is with these Carthinians that they all want to meet Mother? I need to divert Adina's attention until I can meet with Derrik.*

"No! She needs her rest. Why don't we dance? It'll help steer my mind in a different direction," he suggested in a panic and a small amount of disgust.

Adina was elated by his suggestion, and she bounced off the chair and onto the ballroom floor with him.

As they twirled around, Korin made eye contact with his father and gestured discreetly to cut into the dance.

Audun obliged, rose from the table and moved toward them, tapping on his shoulder. "May I? I would like a dance with my pretty daughter-in-law." Adina blushed and gave a small curtsy. Korin moved aside and handed

Adina's hand to his father, and disappeared into the crowd, like the shadow he was.

He tapped a hidden panel in one of the darkened corridors, off the grand ballroom, and hurried down a secret passage until he reached Derrik's lair where he found the Healer working feverishly on his lethal requests.

Derrik was startled when the young Prince popped up next to him.

Where has he come from? The doors are locked, and I haven't heard a knock.

"Y-your Highness, I-I'm not quite finished yet." He looked around to figure out where Korin had come from.

"Don't bother looking. There are many secrets you are not privy to. How much longer?" Korin yelled.

"Maybe another half an hour at best. I can't guarantee it'll work the way it's supposed to because it needs time to boil off," he explained.

"I need it now, and I'll take a chance. Isn't there anything you can do to help hasten this?" Korin asked with banked fury.

"Your Highness, I'm doing my best." Derrik's hands were shaking as he mixed the final ingredients. He was terrified of

Korin—after all, the winds had carried tales of torture to his ears—but the devil of curiosity in him couldn't stand knowing who the concoction was intended for and why the sudden dire need for urgency.

He almost blurted out the question but looked up to see a cold expression settling on Korin's face and restrained himself. He could get to the truth by other means. Dying tonight by the Prince's hands would not help him in any way.

Korin's impatience increased. He paced back and forth for a little while, then sat down on a chair in a dark corner, one leg resting on the opposite knee, with his boot twitching the entire time. He couldn't seem to shake off his nervous energy and sit still. He pulled out his flask and guzzled down the contents. Then he looked around the room, searching for more.

"Where do you keep the brandy?" he asked, tapping his fingers on the armrest of the chair.

Derrik saw the state Korin was in and offered something else instead. "Just a minute, Sire. I have something better." He walked to a shelf and reached for a dusty bottle, wiped it clean with his robe, and poured the contents into a small glass for the Prince.

"What's this?" Korin asked with suspicion.

"It's much better than brandy. It's what you'd asked for...to numb the mind and conscience." He smiled with satisfaction at his creation.

Korin hesitated for a moment, then took the glass from him and gulped the contents down in one swallow. He waited for a moment, but nothing happened. He was about to lash out at him when the effects set in. Tingles started in his extremities and spread through his body. This was followed by a wave of a detached feeling that emerged from the inside out. He was anchored to his body yet separated from it. Soon, there was a layer of numbness covering his entire self, and it felt like nothing could bother him anymore. He felt confident like never before. He cared for nothing and nobody.

Korin sat back down and remained there until Derrik was done.

Finally, the Healer hesitantly handed him the potion in a small glass container and said, "Here you go, Your Highness. Like I said, it may not work the way it was intended, but it's the best I can do under the circumstances."

Korin grabbed the bottle from him and turned to leave.

Derrik couldn't help himself as he shouted out after him, "Dare I ask the recipient of this mixture, Your Highness?"

Korin refused to offer an answer and dashed off.

Derrik remained frozen with curiosity. In all his years as a Healer, he had never been asked to do something like this. He listed in his mind names of possible recipients of the deadly potion, the kingdom's enemies, but shook his head each time crossing them off one by one. In the end, there was nobody left, and he was baffled. Ultimately, he surmised it was probably for the Carnithians. Though the reason the King would invite them for the wedding and kill them off was beyond his powers of understanding.

Korin hurried down the secret passageways until he reached his mother's chamber. He opened the hidden doorway and discreetly caught the attention of a chambermaid, who walked over to him on her tiptoes.

He pressed the glass bottle into her palm, and she looked at it confused. He placed his finger firmly against her lips to indicate silence.

"I need you to give this to my mother," he ordered in whispered tones.

She recoiled and shook her head vehemently, frightened beyond her senses. Korin's hand moved from her lips to her neck, and his other hand grabbed her arm, twisting it behind her back while squeezing her throat. "If you so much as refuse or threaten to tell someone or even look suspicious, I *will cut your throat* and feed your body to the royal dogs. Then I will come for your family and kill them all. Men. Women. Children. Their bodies will never be found. You understand?"

The chambermaid was shocked to silence, and a shiver traversed down her spine. She wondered how he expected her to give the Queen the drink without arousing suspicion. She trembled in fear, knowing Korin would carry out his threat if she refused.

"Your mother won't drink it, Your Highness. She'll become suspicious. She'll want to know what it is," the slight woman pleaded tearfully.

"You'll tell her it's from the high priest. Now go and give it to her and wipe the tears off your face. There's nothing to cry about. This is just a royal duty you're carrying out."

The girl wiped her face and retreated a step, knowing she was about to commit an act of royal treason, but also realizing she had no choice. She had to do this to protect *her* family. She turned around and slowly walked toward Beyla, who was staring out the window with a melancholic expression on her face. A mother missing her precious son desperately.

On the way, the girl uncapped the container and poured the potion into a cup, hiding the bottle in her dress pocket, and approached the Queen. She whispered something to Korin's mother and handed her the cup. They exchanged a short conversation, which Korin couldn't hear from his hiding place, and the Queen smiled sadly. Beyla took a quick glance around the room and drank the contents without protest, then turned around to look out the window.

The chambermaid began to sob quietly, standing behind her. Korin waited to see if the potion took effect. At first, nothing happened, and Beyla continued to stare out, her gaze not faltering. This infuriated him. He was sure the chambermaid was at fault and had alerted his mother, who had pretended to drink from the cup to keep appearances, thus fooling him. And he was nobody's fool. He became enraged with the whole situation and beckoned the nervous chambermaid over to him.

Twisting her arm forcefully, he pried out of her what she had told his mother. "What did you tell the Queen?" he growled low into her ear.

"You're hurting me, Your Highness," she pleaded in anguished tones, keeping her voice low.

"Have you forgotten what I'm capable of? What did you tell her?" He twisted her arm tighter, increasing his grip on her the more she struggled to release herself.

It was then that Beyla collapsed to the floor. A muffled thud drew his attention away from the chambermaid toward his mother, easing his hold on the girl's arm. The girl wrenched herself from his grasp and ran to the Queen, who was lying in a heap on the floor. She kneeled beside her and cried out, looking at Korin briefly, "I told her the truth. And yet she drank it."

Korin was beyond furious. This chit of a girl had openly disobeyed his orders. He rushed toward her and threatened the weeping girl, "If you so much as let a single word escape your mouth, I'll have you beheaded for poisoning the Queen. You understand?"

"Wh-what?" The young girl was horrified by his threat. Terror struck deep into her bones, and the thought of Korin having no misgivings about poisoning his own mother chilled her soul. She mumbled, half-numb in fear, "But… but…I didn't poison her. I tried to warn her. *You* gave it to me…to give it to her."

"Shut up! Who do you think they'll believe? It was your hand that poured the poison into the cup and delivered it to her. I tried to stop you, but not in time. That's how it'll be written and played out in the King's court unless you keep your mouth shut. Killing you will be just as easy," Korin snarled.

The girl's gaze lifted up at him in resignation as his penetrating eyes reaffirmed his threats. She remained fearfully silent and let Korin change the entire narrative of the situation.

He scooped up Beyla in his arms and placed her on the bed. By then, the rest of her staff-in-waiting had hurried over. He asked one of the other maids to call for the Healer immediately.

He sat by the side of his mother's bed and stroked her face, while tears welled in his eyes, going through all the motions of a concerned, loving son. He then picked up the cup and sniffed the contents as if to investigate it.

"What was in this cup? I came up to see my mother as I was told she was indisposed and not feeling well. But when I reached here, I saw her drink the contents of the cup and fall to the ground."

The other ladies-in-waiting murmured among themselves, wondering what was in the cup, then fell silent. They felt deep empathy for Korin. The girl who gave the cup to the Queen sobbed uncontrollably but silently, standing on the other side.

It wasn't long before Derrik arrived. Looking at the gray pallor of the Queen's face, he realized it was his own concoction that had done this. He was shocked to discover who Korin's intended victim was. The Healer was an evil man, no doubt, but nothing could match the level of darkness that was in Korin's heart. Appalled and struggling to come to grips with the truth, he went through his routine of checking for the pulse and feeling for breaths.

After a long examination and inhaling deeply to calm his own nerves, he offered his opinion. "She's barely alive. I can feel the breath pass through her lips and a faint heartbeat, but both are fleeting. Sire, she's on the threshold of death. I'm not sure she can be saved from whatever she's taken."

"Don't say that. You're the Healer. Do something to help her. Surely, there must be something." Tears ran down Korin's face, and Derrik was shocked at his level of acting. The Prince was playing the part of a grieving son who wanted his mother's life saved at any cost.

So, he too played along. Derrik hurriedly rummaged through his bag of evil deeds and pulled out several vials of liquid (containing nothing more than water) and in a somber voice ordered one of the chambermaids to give one to the Queen immediately.

Remaining at her side he said, "I'll give her one every hour and check her breathing. I'll keep you informed. Hopefully, it can combat whatever she's taken and improve, Sire."

"This is all Eyvind's fault. His actions have caused my mother to take her own life." Tears flowed from Korin's eyes freely, and he shook his fists and screamed, throwing nearly a tantrum to convince others of his loss and the "love" he had for his mother. Derrik found Korin overdoing things but kept mum to save his own neck. Luckily, the chambermaids were all innocent who knew nothing about the political winds of Carron, so the Prince was convincing enough not to cast suspicion upon himself.

After minutes of continued rant, he calmed down and excused himself to go to the ballroom to inform his father.

Adina too had been searching for Korin for quite some time when he finally reappeared. She rushed over to him and grabbed his arm. "Where've you been?"

"To see Mother. I've been worried." A quiet answer into her ears and Adina was touched by the level of his caring.

"How's she doing now?"

"She's taken a turn for the worse. I need to see my father."

Just then, Tara rushed over to them. "I would like to pay a visit to Beyla."

Korin didn't like her intrusion, but then his brain went over the plan quickly.

She will make a nice witness to confirm the truth of the Queen's illness and death. And nobody will blame us. Carthinia can do this much for us.

He smirked at the thought and rearranged his facial features. He gave a nod to his approaching father, gesturing for him to play along.

Korin took them to his mother's chamber, and upon reaching it, he ordered all the chambermaids out of the room. The guests stepped in, Audun too, not knowing what to expect. A feeling of distress clutched at Audun's heart, unaware of Korin's actions, but he had to trust his son.

Korin led the group to his dying mother's bedside where she lay listless and pale, unconscious with Derrik at her side. Adina was the first to run to Beyla's side and hold her hand, caressing it gently as she kneeled beside her with tear-filled eyes.

Tara was not touched by this moving scene and her daughter's empathy and remained rigid and unaffected. "What did she succumb to?"

"We're not certain. But it seems nothing can be done for her, according to the Healer," Korin explained mournfully. Derrik sadly nodded.

Tara was finally convinced they were not lying to her; nonetheless, she was still suspicious about the change in wedding plans. Camden remained silent, just observing and paying his respects to the dying Queen.

But it was Audun who was caught in the eye of the storm. This…this was not what he ever expected. The color drained from his face at the sight of his wife lying so motionless. He might not have agreed with his wife's opinions, but death was not what he wanted. His head swirled with memories of happier times when he had been deeply enamored in her and had stolen her away from her people to satiate his own desire to possess her beauty.

He knew his wife had not shared the same desire for him, but she had made peace with her situation and had accepted her fate. She lived her life with him as peacefully as she could, finding her happiness in caring for the people around her.

He was jarred from his memories when a sarcastic voice shoved her opinion upon them. "Pity we're not in Carthinia, because our healers would have a remedy for her in no time at all. Shame, isn't it?"

Both Audun and Korin held their tongues, restraining themselves. Now was not the time to lash out at her callous remark. Camden was less severe in his actions than his wife. He respectfully bowed before Beyla. "I suggest we go out and let her rest."

Tara scowled at him but was pleased she had gotten her jabs in.

The Queen lay dying in the room, while the ceremonies down in the ballroom were concluded somberly for the evening with the announcement that Korin would wed Adina. It came as a surprise to everyone, but the effect of the surplus of the wine drunk inhibited their urge to know the details.

Adina was shocked that nobody was feeling the grief as keenly as she was. She felt like a lone island in the midst of a vast sea of strangers. Korin had become cold and distant toward her since they came down to the ballroom. She tried to console herself that his reticence was due to his mother's dire condition. But something in her was not convinced.

The night finally concluded as Beyla lay facing death on her lonely bed.

RAIDON HURRIED THROUGH THE forest with the horses, occasionally looking up at the sky to see if Aurelius had released the hawks to seek them out. So far, there were none; however, he was taking no chances.

He rode through the rough terrain at a feverish pace, pushing the horses to their limits, and stayed off the known paths as much as possible. Evening approached and he could feel the rays of the setting sun hitting his back. By his estimation, he wasn't too far from the edge of the forest. Now he knew he had to be careful not to release the horses too quickly because he had to give himself enough time to get away without having an extensive search party sent out for him.

He also knew by now, Aurelius would have ordered some men back to Jasper to summon help and search for them. This also meant the hawks would be released anytime to help find the escapees.

The sun sank low below the horizon, and Raidon was about a mile and a half from the edge of the forest. He thought about urging the horses in the direction of Jasper, but at the last moment, he hesitated and figured they would make their own way out of the woods sooner or later.

He released their reins and made a quick departure in the opposite direction. Raidon took advantage of the remaining light to get as deep into the forest as he could, his gaze cast skyward from time to time. The thick canopy of the trees made it difficult to see clearly if he was being sought by the hawks.

On the other side of the forest, the men Aurelius had sent to Jasper to fetch help finally made it to the city by nightfall. They had run the entire way and were out of breath, starved, and thirsty. The castle was winding down the festivities of the evening while the Queen lay dying in her chamber, longing for Eyvind.

Korin, Audun, Derrik, and the high priest were assembled in Beyla's chamber along with Adina, who refused to leave the Queen's side.

The entire place was submerged in gloom and anxiety. Late that night, a soft knock on the door, answered by a chambermaid, let in a soldier with a concerned look on his face, asking for Korin. The Prince went out to speak with the soldier, who informed him of the events that had transpired at the woodcutter's cabin. Korin became panicked at the events.

He entered the Queen's chamber, giving his father a pointed look, and spoke to the others. "I will have to request you to excuse the King and I as there are many details for tomorrow that have to be taken care of."

Adina was miffed and thought it was insensitive of Korin and Audun to both leave Beyla at a time like this to take care of something others could easily do. As the father and son were leaving the room, she got up and walked toward them, looking at Korin in askance. "How can you think of leaving her? Can't someone else take care of *those* details?"

Her betrothed was in no mood to explain anything. Things were not going as planned, and it felt that, at each turn, they were being thrown off course and were facing setbacks they could ill afford.

Audun explained to Adina kindly, "There are a few preparations and rituals that have to be taken care of in case the Queen passes away during the night."

Adina was bold enough to question the King, while looking at Korin in anger, "How can you be so insensitive and despondent? You can't give up. What if she gets well?"

They were taken aback by her comment. Quick thinking was needed to answer her question, without drawing suspicion on themselves.

"You've heard the Healer. I'd love to believe she'd get well, but I have to face the harsh reality that she most probably will not. It may seem cold and callous, but our culture requires certain things to be in place and rituals conducted before a funeral. We have to do these things, despite how painful they are," Audun lied with a straight face, wearing a mask of grief with eyes dulled and lips downturned.

He'd come to terms with what Korin had done and was glad of a complication done away, without his having to do anything about it. Beyla could have created problems for both of them. They needed to plan their next steps to be taken over the following days.

Looking at the King's sad countenance, Adina nodded her head tearfully. "I suppose it is your culture." She reassured herself with the same words repeated in her mind and walked back to sit with the Queen.

And with that, the two men disappeared out of sight, whispering to each other.

"What does he mean by, 'they vanished'? How can someone just vanish? Is this some sort of trickery?" growled Audun in anger, raging outward after the guard gave them the message from the two soldiers.

Korin offered no reply. He too, had the same exact questions.

They both rushed to Audun's chamber, where the two soldiers were interrogated. They answered all the questions fired by the father-son duo.

Audun started pacing the room, then halted suddenly. "We should send out the hawks as well as a large search party. They couldn't have gone too far."

Korin agreed. "Let's send them right away."

"We have to be cautious and not alert the Carthinians. The search party must be disguised as ordinary citizens moving about because Tara and Camden are already suspecting something. We can't afford a single slip-up. We've come too far and worked too hard to fail now," warned Audun.

Korin walked out of the room and ordered a party of forty men dressed as civilians to trickle out in small groups before dawn, together with hunting hounds.

Additionally, he ordered the release of hawks at daybreak to help the soldiers guide and find the prisoners. He couldn't believe Aurelius' incompetence.

"Fool! Fool!" he exclaimed. "What was he thinking? Eyvind should never have been allowed to go with him!"

While all these decisions were being taken care of in the castle, far away from them, Raidon took advantage of the nighttime to head back in the direction of the Talbot Range. It would take him the entire night of travel to reach the mountains early or mid-morning. He was tired, aching in places he couldn't believe existed. The past two days had taken a toll on him. Being hungry and thirsty added to his exhaustion. But stopping was not an option.

He mustered all his strength and fought hard against the body's urges that pleaded with him to stop and take rest. *If I stop now, I will never get back up.* He looked around to get his bearings. The forest was dark and seemed endless, and putting one foot in front of the other was all that he could do.

After an hour or two, his body started betraying him. Exhaustion took over, and strange sounds assailed him from all sides. His mind began to fragment as he heard voices and sounds that weren't really there. His eyes played tricks on him. Occasionally, he saw something from the corner of his eyes as if a shadow was moving about at a distance. He sometimes chased them and oftentimes, ran away from them, not realizing they were nothing more than the tricks of his fatigued mind.

Soon he began to go off track. He wandered through the forest aimlessly in a state of delirium for the rest of the night. It had been at least three days since he last ate something. Finally, he collapsed beneath a gigantic tree, overcome by exhaustion, and it wasn't until the beams of the sun pierced through the branches and danced upon his face that he woke up.

Exhausted and disoriented, he lifted his head and looked around, trying to figure out where he was and what he was doing there. He didn't even recollect who he was. The world was a blur, and his mind was nothing but a foggy mush. He wondered if he were dead. He was half-conscious and too exhausted to think.

He felt his life slipping away bit by bit, as he lay on the ground staring up at the sky. The cold morning air blew on his face. He shivered slightly, but he wasn't fazed by it. His gaze drifted to the high sky where a solitary hawk was surveying the terrain to seek out the foe with precision.

His eyes began to close from following the flight of the hawk until a loud squawk from high above jarred him awake. The squawk felt familiar, but his head was clouded, and he couldn't bring himself to think clearly enough to discern the source. He remained where he lay, fading in and out of consciousness as the squawking continued to draw closer.

In the deepest region of his mind, he knew the sound represented an alarm, but he was too weak and delirious to do anything about it. He just wanted to slip into eternal rest.

Suddenly, a slight surge of reasoning made him aware of the increased squawking. It was the hawks. They had alerted their masters, who would be soon upon him. But he was too weak to fight or even hide. He felt defeated, but he could not allow himself to be captured because that would compromise Eyvind's and Roni's escape. He had to do something.

Fishing for strength from deep within him, he lifted his body slightly and noticed he was under a Boad tree, which produced the "poisonous" berries. He resolved to take his life by ingesting a handful of them, rather than get caught and tortured by Korin for information.

With great effort, he reached for the fallen fruit, gathered a few, and shoved them into his mouth in order to hasten his death. He barely had the energy to crush them to release the "poisonous" juice.

He waited for his life to slip away, but nothing happened. Instead, he became more lucid, and the heavy feeling consuming his body and fogging his mind rapidly dissipated. He couldn't figure out how that could be.

Am I dying? Is this just the process of my soul being released from my body?

With this thought, he touched his face, chest, and the ground, then found himself sitting up with complete ease.

High above, the squawking became still louder. "It's the alarm," he muttered to himself.

Raidon was baffled by his state of being. He didn't know if he was dead or alive. He had just consumed a handful of "poisonous" berries; therefore, he had to be dead. It wasn't long before he heard hounds at a distance charging his way.

He didn't know whether to remain where he was or depart. If he were dead, then the hounds would only come upon a body.

A thought occurred to him. *If I were dead, then my body should be lying on the ground. Yet, here I am. Up and about.*

He was completely mystified by the whole berries' episode. He should have been dead since he knew very well that the Boad tree berries were never to be consumed. Yet he appeared to be alive and invigorated as if the exhaustion of the past twelve hours had never occurred.

His ears picked up the sound of the hunting hounds, and they were not too far, approaching at a fierce pace in Raidon's direction as hawks too continued to circle and alert the soldiers from high above.

Raidon gathered himself and began to run. At first, he wasn't sure where he was because he had wandered aimlessly in his state of delirium during the night. For all he knew, he could just be moments from the edge of the forest or close to Jasper.

He paused for a moment and looked around to get his bearings, but nothing looked familiar. He didn't have much time and needed to act fast. The fall of the shadows crudely helped him determine which direction to run.

Luckily, it was away from the hounds; however, he needed to escape the hawks that were circling above, alerting the soldiers of his every step.

Raidon ran as fast as his legs could carry him, and at the same time, his mind tried to tackle the problem of the hawks hovering above.

Then he remembered the vial Roni gave him. He reached into his pocket and pulled it out, but before he used it, he found dense vegetation in which he could hide so the hawks couldn't catch a glimpse of him.

Raidon carefully opened the stopper and dropped the last remaining bead of fluid onto his head. In a flash, he became invisible. Vanished into thin air.

The hawks soared above, searching for him, but couldn't find him. They flew in wide circles, combing and scanning the ground, but there was no sign of Raidon. He was nowhere to be found.

Raidon ran through the forest at a feverish pace when he heard the dogs approach. Although he was invisible, the dogs could still follow his scent. With the speed and agility of an athlete, he bolted through the forest trying to outrun the hounds. Increasingly, they closed in on him.

Raidon had to think fast.

At a distance, he heard the roar of a waterfall. He was close to the river, and he decided that was where he would lose them. He didn't have much time before the effect of the potion would wear off and the hounds caught up with him. Raidon ran as fast as he could, jumping over boulders, shoving aside branches, and brushing past bushes as he flew through the forest.

The hounds were catching up to him following his scent. He could hear the soldiers on horseback following close behind. He had to get to the water soon if he were to lose them. By now, Raidon was convinced he was quite alive, and to remain alive, he had to conjure up the last bit of energy to make his escape. He glanced back and saw the hounds heading his way at a distance, and not too far away behind them were soldiers on horseback.

The sound of the waterfall was just ahead. However, he had to get to it before they caught up with him. He was certain he would not make it.

Raidon pumped his legs faster and ran with all his might, pushing himself beyond his normal capabilities. But the hounds were faster and nipped at his heels in no time, closing in on him. He could hear their snarling barks right at his feet, but he had no time to look behind.

He could feel their breath brushing against his legs as they snapped their jaws wildly and barked ferociously.

With a burst of adrenaline, Raidon jumped into the air to escape their menacing jaws and leaped over the thick brush, not realizing what lay on the other side of the dense scrub vegetation. He found out soon enough as he fell off a steep cliff and hurled down into the river below.

The hounds came to an abrupt halt at the edge of the cliff and barked incessantly to get the riders' attention.

The soldiers came to a halt and dismounted their horses, peering down the cliff to see where their prisoner or prisoners went. The soldiers released a volley of arrows into the waters below hoping to hit any target. They spread out along the cliff's edge and looked down to see if any heads surfaced, but they saw none.

Meanwhile, Raidon submerged himself in the water and tried to swim downstream to escape them. He was hurt not from an arrow but from the fall itself, which had broken a few of his ribs. His breathing became increasingly hard and labored as the broken ribs pressed into his lungs. He continued to use the fast currents of the river to get as far downstream as he could.

High above on the cliffs, the hounds paced back and forth, searching for the escapees to no avail. Several soldiers continued to shoot arrows into the waters, hoping to hit anyone, not knowing that the current had already carried Raidon away a great distance.

The hawks continued to circle the air and scan the ground rigorously but failed. The water was too rough to reveal any disturbance. The riders and the hounds followed the river downstream for a while to see if any bodies had washed ashore. After a short wait, nobody surfaced. They examined the rough waters and determined that no one could have survived the fall, and even if they had done so, it would only be a matter of time before they succumbed to the injuries they sustained.

Raidon floated to the surface a few miles away and noticed he was still invisible. He gasped to breathe. He opened his mouth to take in a big mouthful of air, yet all he was able to take in was a strangled breath, and ultimately, he couldn't even do that. His lung was punctured. It was just a matter of time before he would die. He could hardly believe his luck. This was the second time he had come so close to death in one day.

Surrendering himself to his fate, he floated downstream as far as the waters could carry him. There were no longer any hawks in sight and no barking hounds. He remained invisible. All sounds of the soldiers faded away into the distance.

Eventually, Raidon was washed ashore, where he lay motionless, gasping to breathe. Each inhale came with more difficulty than the previous one. He clutched the tiny vial in his hand, pulled off the stopper, and tried to shake out the remains into his mouth in hopes of relief. The vial was empty.

By now, his lips had taken on a bluish tint, slowly turning into a dusky shade of death. Raidon was fading away.

"ANY WORD OF THEM?" Korin yelled out impatiently.

"One of the hawks just arrived with a message, Sire," replied one of the soldiers.

The Commander snatched the message from the soldier and promptly passed it to Korin, who read it quietly, his features slowly turning into one of disbelief as he read the words on it. Once, and then a second time.

He looked at the Commander with narrowed eyes. "Fell to their death? How can your soldiers say that?" He passed on the message to the Commander, who read it quietly.

Korin yelled at him, "How can they be certain they're all dead? Did they fetch the bodies out of the water or find them washed ashore?

"The message doesn't mention anything about that, Sire," stated the Commander.

"Idiots!" Korin exclaimed.

The Commander nodded in acknowledgment. "I'll release the hawks again to survey the whole area and find them, dead or alive, Sire," he reassured the young Prince.

Korin was satisfied with the answer, and the Commander excused himself and left the room.

Moments later, a somber-looking chambermaid appeared at the door. Korin knew what the nature of her message would be. She quietly approached him and gave him the news tearfully. "The Queen passed on moments ago, Your Highness."

Korin gave her no reply and remained visibly unaffected. He was numb to his dirty deed.

The messenger wiped the tears from her face and awaited his answer. After a while, she felt awkward standing there, then bowed low, and excused herself.

Korin suppressed the guilt of having murdered his own mother.

Within moments, his father entered the room. "It's time, Korin," he said quietly.

Korin poured brandy into a glass, threw it down his throat, and without uttering another word, they exited the room and made their way to Beyla's chamber.

Sounds of sobbing could be heard as they approached the room.

Korin was surprised to see Adina still at Beyla's bedside, her face puffed up and swollen and her eyes teary and reddened. It was obvious she had been weeping for a while.

Korin bent down and touched his mother's hand. Beyla was pale and cool to the touch. That shocked him. His warm mother with a kind heart was cold and stiff now. He had not given much thought about how he would deal with the consequences of his actions. He was horrified and wanted to get away from it all. As he got up, he swayed on his feet and quickly came to grips when his father grabbed him by the arm and steadied his balance.

To the others, Korin's reaction appeared to be of a bereaved son who had just lost his mother, and no one cast any suspicion upon him. Adina ran into his arms to console him as he continued to stare at his mother's body in utter shock. She muttered words of consolation, but nothing registered in his mind.

After a while, he stepped back from Adina and turned to look at his father. "We need to prepare for the funeral."

Audun nodded, his face an expression of misery. He walked up to Beyla, sat beside her on the bed, then took her small, elegant hand and held it for a moment. He quietly asked her for her forgiveness. Somewhere deep within a chasm and a fold, his love for Beyla still existed even though he knew it had not been mutual.

He had buried his emotions deeper into himself over the years, and yet one act of Korin caused them all to surface. He deeply regretted his actions, feeling a well of remorse and guilt opening up in him. Audun was lost in a sea of memories, and tears made tracks down his cheeks.

Korin went to his father and gently squeezed his shoulder, bringing him back to reality. They had to remain focused on their plan and nothing else. As the circumstances were, they kept running into one setback after another.

Adina rushed back into Korin's arms and sobbed uncontrollably, her behavior annoying him immensely.

What is with her? It is not as if her mother has died. Enough of these tears.

He didn't mouth any of his thoughts but kept them buried within him. The love he had felt for Adina dissipated, and all he could feel now was disgust for this clingy, weepy woman. She was not the strong, self-assured woman with whom he had fallen in love. She had never displayed such frailty or weakness in his presence in the past.

Korin did not know the truth that this was who Adina really was. All the boldness and strength he had admired were no longer present in her because she had been playing a role during all their rendezvous, just to appear mysterious.

But at the moment, he couldn't do anything with the weeping woman other than pretend to be a supportive betrothed.

Soon the bells tolled, and it wasn't long before everyone gathered at the house of worship. The priests dolefully went about their duties of chanting hymns in muffled tones.

The head priest was clad in a white robe with a gold rope belt at his waist. A flowing white cape was draped over his shoulders that cascaded down to his feet. The Carronites wore white funeral garments, signifying the purity of the soul. Their reds were reserved for festivities signifying the blood of life and celebration.

Ushers stood by with white cloaks in their hands, which they draped over the shoulders of everyone in attendance as they stepped in.

Camden and Tara walked in soberly and stood behind Audun and Korin. Adina remained close to Korin, her face crimson from hours of crying. All the other accompanying dignitaries from Carthinia stood behind their King and Queen.

Tara watched the rituals with a bored eye, completely unaffected. Adina started sobbing midway, and Tara rolled her eyes. Her daughter was an emotional fool, just like her father. The more her daughter sobbed, the more disdain Tara felt toward her. She then cast her eyes toward Korin and Audun. Both men maintained their dignity and were in no danger of falling to the ground in a crying heap, unlike her daughter.

I think I like this Carronite culture.

Seeing all the things in the past few days, Tara coveted the culture and richness of the land of Carron. Disengaging her mind from the funeral proceedings with nary a thought or care, her mind ceaselessly worked to formulate a plan to seize control of Carron and rule it with an iron fist. She was jealous of what these Carronites had and coveted everything she set her eyes upon.

There is so much sophistication in them.

It became intolerable that she had nothing compared to them. She had to come up with a plan all on her own if she were to rule both nations. Camden could not be relied upon as a partner in fulfilling her ambitions.

I want this.

ON THE SHORE OF the river, far away, lay a man weakly gasping to take in a breath. The fragile body was clinging to a thin tether of life that was about to break at any moment. Darkness had fallen before his eyes, and he could feel his life slipping away.

After a while, Raidon's breathing became less labored. No more did he struggle to breathe. A pure white light shone down upon him as two gentle faces looked at him while conversing with one another. Raidon could not understand their words. He wondered if he had finally passed into the afterlife. He was certain he had as all his body pains vanished, and his mind seemed to be more at peace.

He stayed motionless but kept staring at the gentle, serene beings. Slowly, his hearing returned, and he could hear their whispered voices. It wasn't until one of them held up the tiny vial Roni had given him that he came to an abrupt conclusion that he might not be dead after all.

He sat up quickly and felt a sharp pain at his side, which immediately rendered him supine. He realized who they were—they were Imen. Not Kenji or Suki, but they were indeed Imen.

One of them placed his hand on Raidon's chest and gestured for him to stay lying down. Raidon looked around to see if he was still close to the river, but he couldn't hear the rushing waters. He was probably elsewhere in the forest.

The Imen holding the vial bent down and spoke to him, "Where did you get this?"

In a dilemma, Raidon didn't know if he should reveal the entire story, but he was too weak to think up a lie. Besides, they had saved his life and deserved the truth. With apprehension, he slowly told them how he came to possess it.

Their eyes rounded, and both covered their mouths in shock. "Roni? Banished?" They were horrified at this knowledge.

"Yes. And now I am a hunted man and have to reach Roni and Eyvind."

The Imen nodded and stepped back to discuss the situation in private. They returned to him. "We'll help you escape this forest, but not beyond that. Our rules forbid it."

Raidon was relieved and overjoyed. This would aid him in joining his friends. He rushed to get up, but both shook their heads.

"Remain still and allow the healing to complete. Your ribs need to fuse together. It will take around fifteen minutes before we can remove the warm poultice from your chest."

Raidon agreed and took slow deep breaths. He could feel the pain waning. And soon there was nothing. He was as good as he was before; in fact, better than before. He sat up with ease and looked around. "Where are we?"

"Not too far from where we found you," replied one of them.

"Do you know Kenji and Suki?"

"Yes, we do. But how do *you* know them?" the Imen asked in astonishment.

Raidon started from the beginning and told them the entire story but kept Roni's destination a secret from them. His instinct was telling him the place was supposed to be a secret that only the banished knew.

The two Imen were astonished and promised to help him as much as they could without breaking any of their own laws.

Raidon took a deep sigh of relief. His thoughts moved to Roni and Eyvind and if they ever made it to Bellwin or even to the White Forest safely.

Raidon and the Imen started walking in a southernly direction, moving carefully through the rough terrain with Raidon looking up at the sky frequently to see if the hawks were circling.

The Imen noticed his strange preoccupation with keeping a skyward vigil.

"Is there something in the sky?" asked one.

"Hawks. The soldiers from my kingdom release hawks to search. I'm sure they will send one for me."

"Do you see one?" asked the other Imen.

"No. Not at this time. But we do need to worry about them. It's just a matter of time before they appear."

The pair looked up and saw nothing but stopped in their tracks and closed their eyes. They went into a meditative trance and remained in that state of immobility for a few minutes.

Raidon knew they were doing something wonderful to help him but didn't know what it was exactly. When they were done, and opened their eyes, he asked politely, "May I ask what you were doing?"

The first one looked at him with a gentle smile and answered, "They won't be searching for you anymore."

Raidon believed what they said but was curious to know what exactly they had done. But he remained silent, voicing his words only in his thoughts.

How does it matter anyhow? They've come through every single time in the past.

The trio began their trek through the forest up to the southern edge, hurrying as fast as they could until they came upon a huge Boad tree that reminded Raidon of the morning's episode when he had eaten the "poisonous" berries.

"Today was the first time I got to know that the berries are filling and non-poisonous," he told them of his experience.

"Poisonous? No. No. They are actually life-sustaining and help you not feel hungry for a long time. Even those who are starving to death will find their energy replenished by eating them."

Raidon reached up, pulled off a handful of berries, stuffed them into his pockets for later, and then hurried past the tree. He was disgusted at the lies that were passed down the generations.

Hurrying through the forest, they finally came to an area where the trees were less dense, and it was then the Talbot Range came into view at a distance. All three were relieved.

Raidon took one last look at the sky out of sheer habit.

"Don't worry. They won't follow you," reassured the Imen.

"I've reached my destination," stated Raidon with relief. "I can manage from here. Thank you once again for everything you've done for me." He saw no point in their escorting him further, so he bid them farewell, taking care not to tell them where exactly Roni had gone.

The Imen stopped and obliged without argument. As they were about to leave, he asked for the empty vial so he could return it to Roni. He also asked them to give a message to Kenji and Suki that he and Eyvind would make sure Roni was safe.

The Imen handed him the vial and said their goodbyes. "Travel safe." They moved in the opposite direction and suddenly vanished.

Raidon stared at the place they were a moment ago, then moved hastily toward the mountain. He recalled Roni telling them about the white flower trail, so he scanned the ground to search for it. It took a while before he could see one or two, then a few more, and soon his sharp eyes found a distinct pattern. It was only visible if one paid close attention and was astute enough to realize they marked a trail. If Roni had not mentioned it, Raidon was sure he could never have figured it out.

The white flowers led him to the huge cascade of rocks from where they had retrieved the *callioux*. He walked in the direction of it and made his way to the sheer smooth face of the cliff. It was an intimidating sight as the mountain range rose almost vertically before him, and he couldn't see many crevices he could use to climb up. One slip and a certain death awaited below. The smooth cliffside reminded him of the walls of Jasper that had stopped their enemies from attack many times.

Radon lifted his arms and found the first niche to support his weight. Soon he began his climb, feeling for the fissures and cracks to pull himself up. He kept a close watch on the skies for the hawks and below at the ground for the soldiers. So far, he was safe from spying eyes or hunting soldiers.

He kept his concentration focused on his climb, his hands growing slippery from profuse perspiration. He kept drying them on his clothes before he went to grip the next crevice but within moments, they were moist. Such were the hardships of climbing a mountain range that took no prisoners.

He was only about halfway up when his fingers started trembling and his grips began to fail due to exhaustion. He decided to rest for a moment by hanging on to the sheer rock face with the tips of his fingers. That required a lot of energy, and eventually, his left hand too slipped off, but his other hand and left foot bore the weight of his body, and his sheer determination kept him upright, clinging to the mountain wall.

He reminded himself to be prepared to slip again and always have at least one toehold and one hand, preferably of the opposite limbs, in a strong position before reaching for the next niche.

He had never climbed a mountain before, and he was learning on the go, using his common sense. His left foot and right hand had to have a strong hold and remain secure in order for him to raise his left hand to feel for the next crack higher up, and then find a strong toehold for his right foot to push himself up.

And then repeat the whole action by reaching up with his right hand and then bringing the left foot up. This right-left combination seemed to conserve the most energy while climbing the tortuous mountain face.

He ascended a few feet, and then his left foot slipped off its spot and dangled in the air. Luckily, using his alternate method, he held himself rigid while patiently searching for a strong toehold again to push himself up.

At every point, the mountain seemed to deter his climb. Raidon searched the smooth cliff for a crevice to secure his hand but could find only tiny areas that were insufficient to grab and pull himself up. And even if he managed to get his foot and hand into good spots, they only held on to the mountain for a few seconds before slipping off. That made it impossible to rest for long. The only way to rest was to continue climbing up using opposite limbs and giving his body quick respite between each ascent.

Evening was approaching quickly, and he needed to reach the top before he ran out of light and strength. Things were bad enough as they were, with his hands getting cut and oozing blood.

He looked down again to check if he could catch a glimpse of any movement in the forest, indicating the position of the soldiers or Aurelius. There was no one in sight so he continued to feel around to get to his next grip.

Inch by inch, he made his way up, taking his time to find the strong spots. His right hand gave way when he broke another fingernail and so also his feet, and he dangled from the mountain, facing his death. Eventually, he righted himself once again. With the growing shadows, he was unable to see the hidden niches and missed many of them.

It was slow going, and with the sun setting, the magical light of the dusk blanketed the surroundings. He looked up to see how much distance he had to cover to reach the top and was disheartened when he realized he still had some climb ahead of him, and the mountain looked insurmountable. A strong drive to survive this climb consumed him, and he made a promise to himself that he would not die in vain.

He had reached almost to the top when darkness shrouded the land completely. He couldn't see the rock face in front of him. It was then he heard sounds at a distance below. The soldiers were heading to the mountain range.

I have to reach the top even if the soldiers are standing right below and shooting arrows at me. Nothing is going to stop me from reaching Eyvind and Roni.

He doubled his attempts and used all his might to pull himself up strongly. The tips of his fingers bled and made the going more slippery. They could hardly bear his body weight as pain shot down his arms each time he attempted to do so. He put the pain out of his mind and stopped focusing on it. He recalled all the lessons he had learned as an Imperial Knight and used them on this mountain range.

By now, the soldiers were visible, and he could hear their voices. Their dark shadows moved like tiny ants below under the light of the moon. They were yet not too close to where he was making his ascent. Raidon was not prepared to take any chances.

Then he heard the hounds at a distance. That made him nervous as the dogs would lead the soldiers in his direction. He shook away his fear and kept his energy focused on his climb, his determination stronger than ever.

The dogs finally arrived at the bottom. They sniffed the rocks thoroughly, then pointed their noses up the cliff, and barked relentlessly. Within moments, the soldiers rushed over and searched for the escapees, but it was too dark to see anything.

Raidon could not make out what they were saying, but their actions indicated they were in a hurry to gather firewood. Soon torches twinkled far below in the darkness. The soldiers waved them frantically against the rock wall, but the light barely illuminated anything. Frustrated with the shadows, they shot fire-lit arrows to light up the sheer section of the wall. Meanwhile, the dogs continued to bark viciously.

Raidon used every last bit of energy to pull himself up as fast as he could before his position was given away. The chaos below was distracting, but he continued upward with bleeding hands and busted fingernails and trembling calves.

The pain was unbearable. He wondered if this climb had an end. It almost appeared to be a trick of the mind. The more he climbed, the more there remained to be climbed. He was exhausted.

Blazing arrows were shot high into the dark sky as they whistled and cut through the air, lighting up some parts of the rockface. They struck the mountain and splintered into a burst of sparks like fireworks. The dogs leaped up and thrashed against the rock, snarling and barking in excitement.

Meanwhile, Raidon continued to ascend inch by inch. Finally, his hands felt loose dirt and a flat surface.

"Have I finally reached the top?" he asked himself in disbelief.

He stretched his neck out as far as he could to get a glimpse of where he was.

Yes, he was really at the top. He had indeed conquered the sheer face of the Talbot Mountain Range.

Raidon pulled himself up, using the last reserves of the energy he could muster, and hurled his body onto the flat ground. He lay there wheezing, with the wind knocked out of him.

Far below, he could still hear the whistling of the arrows striking and shattering against the mountain wall. The frantic barks of the hounds and the calls of the soldiers continued. He lay there for only a moment until he caught his breath.

Finally, he rose to his feet and looked over the edge to see how many brave souls were going to attempt the ascent. There were none to be seen.

PURSUIT

Raidon looked around and estimated he needed to move in the southeast direction. The darkness made it difficult to make out any landmarks. The only thing visible was a wall of thickets that ran along the ridge, extending in both directions.

Raidon was too exhausted to move any further, and being unaware of the terrain, he chose to remain hidden in the thicket until daybreak. He knew the soldiers would not dare to make the climb during the night. And even the few who dared would die or not know how to proceed further.

Raidon began to prepare for sleep. Occasionally, he heard distant sounds from far below. Once in a while, he heard the screams of soldiers falling to their deaths from their tenuous attempts to scale the sheer mountain wall in the pitch darkness of the night. Eventually, they too stopped.

Raidon was confident they had given up on attempting the dangerous climb which promised death to most. He was sure they would not succeed in making it to even one-third of the way up in the night.

Tired and weakened, he finally fell asleep as even the rough, jagged surface of the ground became indiscernible to him.

MEANWHILE, THE PREVIOUS NIGHT, Roni and Eyvind had reached the top with great difficulty, but before making a foray into a strange, probably dangerous, territory to find the White Forest, they decided to rest for the night amid the thickets that were growing along the edge of the cliff.

Although they were afraid of being followed by Aurelius' soldiers to the top of the mountain range, the fear of venturing into an unknown land at nighttime was far greater.

Roni lay her head down on a bed of leaves and looked around. It was hard to see in the dark, as the terrain presented itself as a strange barren wasteland under the waxing moon. Eyvind stayed up most of the night to keep watch as Roni slept.

Throughout the night, he was gripped with waves of worry for his mother. He feared for her safety, but there was nothing he could do for her. Sighing deeply to shake off his anxiety, he walked around and focused on keeping them safe.

The night eventually passed uneventfully, and at dawn, when the skies were just getting painted with streaks of pink and orange, he managed to catch some sleep.

As the sun rose and its rays fell upon their eyelids, they got up and looked at their surroundings and the actual makeup of the landscape. An austere dry place it was, in shades of gray and brown, with strange outcroppings of immense gray boulders that protruded from the ground as if the earth had heaved them up from deep within its belly.

At places, there grew gnarled, tortured trees devoid of much greenery. Dried brown leaves hung from some branches, waiting for their turn to fall down. The ground was mostly dirt with a few patches of low-growing, coarse dry grass. Nothing else seemed to exist there.

Roni and Eyvind felt more alone than they were before. Looking at the sun, they plotted their direction and walked southeast where the White Forest was purported to be. With not many places to hide in case they were attacked, they made haste and did not stop to take a break, determined to reach the forest as fast as they could.

As they made their way across the alien surface, they noticed there was not a single clue that implied the place was inhabited by anyone.

"Are we really in Bellwin, Eyvind? There seems to be not a soul in sight."

Eyvind shrugged his shoulders. This was a new land for him. "Seems very unusual, indeed. Let's look around."

They both peered at the ground in search of some sort of indicators. Faint trails marked the terrain. Some of the larger rocks had strange inscriptions carved upon them as if leaving clues only for those who knew how to decipher them.

They explored the area further to check if they could spot any signs of habitation, but none came into view.

"I think trying to find people who can help us is a waste of time. No one seems to be around. Let's stay focused on reaching the White Forest and nothing else," Eyvind urged as the brave souls made their way across the Barren land. Little conversation took place between the two as they concentrated on putting one foot in front of the other.

Berries and other small fruits, from their pockets, became their source of nourishment when they stopped to rest. Roni stared at Eyvind, deeply appreciating his sense of loyalty and commitment even toward a stranger like her. She was in awe and at the same time worried about his future.

"What's to become of you now? You're a fugitive, and so is Raidon." She was sad for both of them, as she was the harbinger of their fates, and she couldn't forgive herself for bringing about such a tragic turn of events.

Eyvind shrugged and continued eating. He had no reply for her.

"I'm sorry for everything that's happened." Her eyes grew teary as her heart filled with remorse.

"You mustn't blame yourself. Look at it this way. You saved me from getting married to someone who's in love with my brother." He smiled, hoping to lighten the conversation.

Her eyes rounded, and her brows arched in surprise. "Oh. How did that come to be?"

"That's the way things sometimes are. Everything is an arrangement of some sort to benefit someone or the other."

"But you gave up your right to the throne," she murmured, as none of it made any sense to her. The world above the ground really seemed to be a strange place.

"And you gave up Imen-Hera," he countered. "Besides, I have no regrets."

Roni was speechless. His words made her think.

Do I have any regrets? I loved my life in Imen-Hera. It was happy. I had my parents and my friends. So many smiles and laughs we shared. I wonder what Kenji and Suki are doing now. And how Mother is coping with it.

Thinking about her parents made her sad and forlorn. Tears filled her beautiful hazel eyes, and the spark in them dimmed.

Eyvind's heart wrenched, seeing the rivulet of tears down her cheek. He realized she was homesick and missing her people. Feeling helpless, he moved closer and wrapped his arms around her, holding her tightly against his chest.

Roni's body stiffened at this contact, and her natural instinct was to pull away until she began to feel and hear his heart beating strongly and at a steady rhythm against her ear. She relaxed and sank deeper into his embrace, finding solace. It felt comfortable and natural to be held by him and comforted. Though strange and new, it was quite nice.

Feeling her arms tentatively glide around him, Eyvind felt peace invading him. He had no regrets about the events that had transpired in his life, except for one thing. His mother. He was consumed by his thoughts about her and felt a gut-wrenching emotion deep in his belly that made him sick to the core. Something was happening at Carron.

They stayed in the same position for a few minutes when Roni spoke up, pointing to a boulder with strange inscriptions etched on it. "I wonder what that means…"

"Not sure. Never seen such inscriptions before. Have you?"

Roni shook her head and stayed silent. They appeared to be ancient writings from long ago, seeing the weathered rock and the cracks on it. Those words might have held profound meaning at one time but had gotten lost now.

Roni leaned away from Eyvind, and both stood up and continued to move forward, not straying from their path. They were puzzled by the lack of civilization on this side of the Talbot Range, a fact that bore heavy on their minds as it gave them a sense of impending danger.

"It's just so strange there's no one in sight. Not even a bird or a worm," remarked Roni, looking around.

Eyvind nodded. "Yes. Very eerie. This is a land of mysteries; however, we don't have time to solve them. I wonder if there's an easier way to Bellwin from another direction."

"No. This is the only way to reach Bellwin. The land on the east is plagued by swamps, bogs, and quicksand. Further west from here is a sheer drop down into the sea," she replied with certainty, shocking herself, as this information had entered her head spontaneously.

"How do you know all this?" Eyvind asked in amazement.

"I'm not sure. I too am wondering the same." Roni was bewildered by this fact also.

"Anything else we should know about before we continue forward? Such as the dangers that may be lurking?" asked Eyvind, scanning the deserted landscape.

Roni concentrated hard, hoping to get some images in her mind, and stared into nowhere. She started to shake her head to indicate they were safe when she stilled suddenly.

The color drained away from her face, and her eyes grew large and filled with terror. Her body stiffened as she became petrified with fear.

Eyvind grabbed her by the arms and looked into her eyes.

"What happened, Roni? What is it?" Her sudden rigidity as she stared ahead frightened him.

Shivers coursed up and down her spine, and her throat seized up. No words passed her lips, and her face was a mask of sheer terror.

"What is it, Roni?" he asked again in anxiety. He shook her gently to snap her out of this trance and speak to him. "Roni! Roni!"

She finally broke out of her fearful daze and looked straight into his eyes. The dread of what was to come communicated directly to his soul, and he broke out into a sweat.

Her lips trembled, but not a single word escaped her quivering mouth.

"What is it?" he pleaded with her.

"A De-demon...a Demon storm," she stumbled over her words.

Eyvind was baffled, having never heard of such a thing. "A Demon storm? What's that?"

Roni fished out a string of sanity from within herself to answer him as her eyes stared again into nowhere. "It's not just a storm but a whirling specter siphoning everything in its path and shredding all of them to bits." She wished these visions would disappear from her head, but they replayed over and over in a loop.

Eyvind looked around in all directions and was perplexed. He could see no evidence of the Demon wind that Roni was describing. *Maybe this is why this land is devoid of living creatures, and there is only silence surrounding us.* He grew worried.

Roni, on the other hand, couldn't seem to shake off the fear that was vibrating within her. Being petrified and standing frozen in terror was not the solution. Taking deep breaths, her inner panic began to abate, and she started thinking more rationally. She realized they needed to hasten and reach the White Forest as fast as they could. Maybe then they would miss the Demon wind. Eyvind too came to the same conclusion.

She grabbed his hand, and both ran as fast as they could across the strange land with twisted trees and eroded boulders, keeping a watch for the specter wind. She breathlessly explained that the monstrous wind whirled around while sweeping the land continuously and agitatedly, relentless in its attack. That made it impossible for anything to inhabit the land and thrive here. It was going to be just a matter of time before it made its way in their direction. They had to be prepared for it.

As Eyvind looked around, he found the clues in the Barren landscape, which was dotted with the tortured bent trees, wind-beaten and stripped of their foliage. Their roots had dug firmly into the ground like talons, refusing to let go of the arid land. And that was how they had survived the ceaseless assaults of the wicked phantom storms for hundreds of years.

The two tore across the landscape that looked the same in all directions, hoping to catch sight of the White Forest. Eyvind was unsure whether they were heading toward the right place. "I hope the White Forest is up ahead somewhere and not behind us," he blurted out, gasping.

Roni simply nodded, not knowing what to say as she too was clueless. They needed to get to the forest before the evil swirling winds appeared, or at least, to a safe place to hide. As they continued to run, they felt a sudden change in pressure, and the air became electrified. There was a strange buzzing sound in their ears. They halted and turned to look behind.

Far off in the distance, they saw the specter funnel forming, looking like a raging bull, full of fury and aggression. It was building speed as it zigzagged across the terrain, preparing to unleash its fury upon them. It picked the land clean of debris as it swept back and forth like a well-choreographed dance.

Roni and Eyvind looked at the wind funnel and then at one another and, without hesitation, ran as fast as their legs could carry them. They looked back occasionally to avoid its path, but the devil of a storm appeared to have a life of its own. The whirling winds glided forward and backward, teasing them. It was preparing itself to ram into them and leave behind only their lives in shreds.

"We should find some shelter for us or something we can anchor ourselves to," Eyvind screamed, trying to be heard above the sound of the gales. They looked all around, but the land offered no such sanctuary.

The skies grew dark, as if the winds had swallowed the sun, and the temperatures fell considerably. They felt the Demon vortex heading straight for them. Dust and debris filled the air, making it difficult for them to see what lay ahead. But that didn't stop them from running, pushing their bodies to the limits, in an attempt to outrun the specter force.

The angry Demon wind grew ferocious and picked up speed, dancing across the Barren surface, until it was aiming straight for them as if recognizing them to be the intruders. No matter how hard they tried to dodge it, it remained intent on its path.

Heaps of debris smashed into them, making them stumble, and they knew it was only a matter of moments before they would be carried off into the biting winds and shredded to bits.

A glance behind and they realized darkness was upon them, encroaching fast. They started to succumb to the Demon winds as the conditions made it difficult for them to run. Struggling to take a step forward, they kept trying, but the swirling gusts made it impossible to budge. They held on to each other and used their unified strength to move, but that too didn't work. They were frozen in one place, soon to be dragged backward as the winds pulled at them.

This was it. The furious specter wanted to destroy them, and nothing would stand its way.

Fear seized Roni at the prospect of being engulfed by the winds. Eyvind shielded her face by burying it into his chest and then covered her head with his hands. He looked around to see if there was something they could hold on to, but the dust and detritus made it impossible to see anything.

"Let's drop to the ground and try to feel for a tree trunk or a root to cling to," he suggested, screaming the words into her ear.

They carefully crouched down and felt around for anything that was anchored firmly to the ground, but the intensity of the winds increased, and an angry force attempted relentlessly to haul them off the ground and drive them into its awaiting mouth.

They clung to each other as tightly as they could, but soon their legs began to lift off the ground, and Roni shrieked in terror. Suddenly, the ground beneath them gave way, and they fell through into an underground cavern.

"Bolt it quickly!" came a shouting command.

Roni and Eyvind tumbled down and came to rest on a dusty floor. Scrambling to their hands and knees, they sat up to see what had just occurred. They were in a cave below the ground surrounded by a few strange-looking, gaunt men, who paid little attention to them but were transfixed by something above.

"Is it bolted tight?" shouted one of the scrawny brutes, who appeared to be in charge.

The other man at the bolt nodded to indicate his affirmation, but all their gazes remained focused on the trapdoor above. No one spoke after that.

They nervously stared up at the hatch and waited. And it wasn't long before a thunderous roar from above battered the ground and shook the trapdoor violently. Fine dust exploded on them as the bolt rattled and the door wobbled. The band of savages stepped back to avoid the dust, but their gazes remained fixed on the trapdoor. No one spoke a single word. It was as if they were frozen in time. Roni and Eyvind too remained silent, not knowing how to react.

The rumble of winds strengthened to a deafening roar as the trapdoor continued to rattle violently. There was a time when Roni thought it would be torn off its heavy hinges and reduced to splinters by the specter.

Meanwhile, everyone below the trapdoor remained still, frozen in time, even as the loud battering continued relentlessly for a long while. It was as if the Demon wind knew they were below and refused to give up on its prey. Still, no one moved an inch. Not even a twitch of the muscle. They were as if carved in stone.

The Demon hammered the door and pounded it hard, beating against it with all its strength until it lost its momentum, and the loud rattling started to subside.

Eyvind and Roni began to get up, but the man in charge raised his hand and gestured for them to stay put without looking at them. They complied. Though they were grateful for being rescued, they didn't know whether these men were friends or foes.

Once the trapdoor stopped shaking, the gaunt men broke out of their trance and turned their attention to Eyvind and Roni, taking in their rich and healthy appearance with great amazement. From the wonder seen on their faces, it was obvious these men had not seen well-dressed strangers pass through their land in a very long time.

Their eyes gleamed with an expression that both were not able to decipher. Roni and Eyvind were not sure of their intentions and if they would be perceived as intruders or simply passersby. They stayed quiet and used caution, trying to get a read of the situation without uttering a word.

The leader approached them. "Who are ye an' wot are ye doin' 'ere?" His gruff voice carried a hint of hostility.

Both Eyvind and Roni didn't know these men were remnants of a race that had inhabited the land above for eons. After pillaging the land, they were cursed with a wind that drove them underground. They were initially large in troops until most were carried off to their deaths by the ferocious whirling winds, and the remaining survivors built a series of tunnels and caverns underground in which they had learned to survive.

But life had been harsh to them. Even below, many had died from starvation, and those who survived were forced to adapt to an austere lifestyle, scavenging for roots and rodents that lived beneath the ground.

Once in a while, they accosted unassuming strangers, who scaled the sheer cliffs of the western borders from the waters below, and stole their provisions. But those too were extremely rare.

Lack of food and an unforgiving life made them gaunt and emaciated, with their bones sharp and protruding. They had yet to come across a passerby who was as beautiful as Roni. Even in her dust-encrusted state, she shone like a jewel amongst the crowd of dirty skeletal thugs. And they were enamored, quickly encircling Eyvind and Roni.

Both became alarmed but tried not to show it, schooling their faces into a mask of friendliness. "We come in peace and mean no harm. We're just passing through on our way to Bellwin, and we're grateful you saved our lives," Eyvind spoke sincerely, using all his training in diplomacy.

"To Bellwin, ye say?" laughed out the leader. The others joined him in bursts of laughter.

Eyvind and Roni became unsettled by their behavior but remained calm. They could feel trickles of fear traversing down their spines. They were too vulnerable in this underground vault with no route of escape, however brave they were.

"Yes. Bellwin," repeated Eyvind, withholding all other information. He didn't want to provide them with anything they could use against them.

"And wot's the nature of yer business in Bellwin?" the leader asked with an ugly grin.

By now, Eyvind and Roni realized they were in danger and needed to think fast. These were not soldiers, but unrefined savages clad in drab and tattered loose-fitting attire. Dust and dirt were encrusted on their weather-beaten faces, and their unwashed bodies and matted hair stank to high heavens. They were filthy.

Looking for an escape route, Eyvind's eyes darted all around the cavern. But all he could perceive were dark shadows. The leader smirked at them, showing off his crooked but sharp yellowish-brown rotted teeth, and leaned forward. Roni wanted to recoil from him but remained steadfast, as did Eyvind. Then, the rest of the six fiends closed in on Roni, their gazes gliding up and down her body, with crude sounds emanating from their throats. It was obvious they had never seen a more beautiful face. Ever!

Their bony hands reached out to touch her, and although her first instinct was to recoil, she stood her ground. One of the emaciated ruffians stepped forward until he was standing uncomfortably close to her.

"She's pretty," he commented lustfully, licking his lips, and raised his hands to reach for her face.

"Get away from 'er!" yelled the leader, kicking the gaunt man.

The man fell backward onto the floor and remained there, cursing under his breath. The rest of the brutes stared at her lasciviously.

Eyvind grew nervous, his hand instinctively reaching for the sword that was normally strapped to his waist. But he got nothing. His renouncement of the throne had stripped him of his weapons.

He wasn't certain how he was going to fight all seven without a weapon. Diplomacy and bargaining would have to do the trick, their only salvation.

"Look, we mean no harm. We'll leave peacefully and continue on our way to Bellwin. We're indebted to you for saving us," he uttered calmly, trying to diffuse the situation that could get volatile at any time.

"You're in Bellwin, you nitwit," roared one of the haggard scoundrels, laughing at him condescendingly.

Roni and Eyvind looked at each other in shock, their minds asking the same question.

If this is Bellwin, then where is the White Forest?

The leader of this band of misfits yelled out, "It's nice to indebted 'n all, but 'ow's we to collect this debt?" He spat on the ground and neared them. "I mean we don't even know who ya're or if we'll 'ver see you again. Right, lads?"

His words roiled the others and caused a wave of agitation to spread amongst them.

"Right!" they hollered in unison.

"You have my word," pleaded Eyvind.

"Your word? Wat does t'at cost?" The leader pushed Eyvind backward, who stumbled a few steps but tightened his torso to keep himself from falling.

"We ain't interested in debts or words, are we, lads? We're starved!" the leader bellowed, pulling his scruffy tunic up to his chest to expose his skeletal rib cage and a sunken abdomen.

"I 'aven't eaten in a while as you can see 'ere. So, debts an' words aren't going to take away me 'unger pains. Understood? What provisions are ye carryin' besides the lovely lady?"

Another skin-and-bones lout jumped forward and tried to grab Eyind's tunic to reach into his pockets.

Eyvind stepped back and firmly kept him away by holding out his hand. He had no more bargaining cards left. The winds had changed and not in their favor. A tight frown creased his forehead as he became increasingly worried about Roni. He had never imagined being in such a dreadful situation.

Roni surreptitiously reached into her pocket and pulled out some Boad berries. She then lifted her arm and held them out on her palm as an offering.

Seeing a bluish glint, one of the men leaped forward and knocked the berries right out of her palm and then flipped her hand over to reveal her sparkling blue ring. His eyes grew wide with greed, and he tried to pry it off her finger, leaving scratches behind.

"Ow! No!" Roni screamed, but the words had no effect on the man. The ring had also caughtthe others' attention. It had been years since the men had seen something so shiny, and they wanted it at any cost.

Eyvind shoved the man away and pushed Roni behind his back, wanting to protect her. The cretins encircled them completely and closed in on them from all sides. Roni and Eyvind had just mere moments to protect themselves.

Roni was mortified by the whole episode and quite aghast at the way that men above the ground behaved (as opposed to Imen-Hera). This was a rude lesson of life teaching her new ways. She had to do something. But what?

Just then she remembered the strange weapons she was carrying on her person. She grabbed the zoon from her hip and swung it around fiercely and, at the same time, handed the *dandum* sticks to Eyvind. She didn't know if he knew how to use them, but surely, something was better than facing the men with his bare hands.

She spun lightly on her feet, and with their backs against one another, they circled around, their eyes focused and shoulders firm, daring anyone to step forth.

What would have caused Eyvind's enemies to pause and take a moment to gather their strategies had no effect on this gang. They were unfazed by the display of the strange weapons.

One of them surged toward Roni, whose years of dance training had taught her to move at lightning speed. She instinctively whipped the zoon fast and aimed it low. It wrapped tightly around both of his legs, and with a swift tug of the zoon, the lout fell to the ground, his back slamming hard.

Eyvind's neck swiveled to take in the fallen man, and his eyebrows rose in surprise at the skill displayed by her. *Oh, I'm impressed. She's full of surprises.*

But that was the only respite the two of them got. The rest of the misfits charged toward them in unison, but before they could get too close, the spinning *dandums* and the whipping zoon brought them to a halt.

Roni looked at Eyvind from the corner of her eye. *So, he does know how to use the dandum. A swift learner is he.*

She swirled her zoon, and the hard ball at the end of the rope whisked past the men's head menacingly. It would take one strike…just one strike…to render anyone unconscious or worse.

The men retreated. Despite facing the harshest of circumstances, they had a strong kernel of survival instinct still vibrating in them. But nothing could beat the pursuit of greed.

A skeletal figure produced a blade and held it in front of them, slashing the air a couple of times to threaten Roni and Eyvind. The man tried to jab at them, but with one hard strike of the dandum stick, Eyvind knocked the knife out of his hand. Using his foot, Eyvind pulled the blade toward him and away from the thug while continuing to wield the dandum sticks.

Next came the leader who used some hand movements to gesture to his men. He wanted to try to distract Roni and Eyvind with a bargain, and just as they let their guards down, his men would pounce on the two of them. The miscalculation was he didn't take into consideration that he was dealing with the young prince of Carron, who had been trained by the best and who knew all the moves ever known to man. A superior fighter that he was, Eyvind could understand the leader's strategy easily and was three steps ahead.

The scrawny motley crew waited for an opportunity to strike them both.

The leader spoke up placatingly. "Wait! Wait! This is no way to treat our guests, is it, men? Where be yer manners? Wot woz yer tryin' to give us, miss?"

Eyvind and Roni knew he was just trying to distract them so he could take them by surprise. They paid no attention to his blabber.

"Like I said, we're passing through and mean no harm. Now, open that door and let us out," Eyvind stated with firmness.

"Now, wait a minute. I said I woz sorry to 'ave come on so rough. Ye 'ave to understand that me men ain't never seen anythin' so beautiful. Can you 'ardly blame 'em?"

Eyvind was not taken in by this show of camaraderie or amused by his phony excuses and knew this was a stalling method. They needed to leave immediately.

"I need you to open the hatch and step aside. You understand?" he restated.

The leader again tried to spew excuses, but his nonsense was truncated by Eyvind's quick approach toward the trap door, with Roni at his back.

The gaunt hoodlums hurried to stop them from getting away.

"Now open it and step away!" shouted Eyvind to a skeletal fiend.

The man refused to comply.

Eyvind struck him in the chest with the dandum stick and shoved him hard. The goon fell to the ground with tremendous force and never got back up.

Roni and Eyvind now wielded their weapons with the intention to maim the next man who approached them. They were growing weary of these back-and-forth moves.

A few of the brave men scampered toward the trap door to prevent them from getting away. But the effect of zoon and dandum made a couple lay on the ground.

"Get away from there!" Eyvind warned. The force and the intensity of his voice were ominous. The rest of the men scattered away, looking at each other and their leader, seeking signs of their next move.

But Eyvind and Roni were too strong as contenders. They were not going to be taken easily. They corralled the men away from the trap door and positioned themselves below it.

Roni reached for the heavy metal rod and unlatched the door. With a swift tug on the rope, the door fell open with a loud thud against the steep ramp that allowed easy access in and out.

During all this, they kept their eyes firmly planted on the ruffians, ensuring they didn't move an inch. Eyvind motioned Roni to climb out first. As she was doing so, he glanced up at the opening, and taking advantage of this distraction, several men rushed forward in his direction. Eyvind wielded the dandums with a deft hand, twirling them with deadly fury and calm focus on the men in front of him, threatening to kill the first person who got close.

The men didn't know how to act. They stared at him anxiously, fearing him, but at the same time, they were not prepared to let the two targets leave so easily.

Roni peered down from the opening and offered her hand to Eyvind to climb up. Eyvind took one last look at the louts in front of him and, with a burst of speed, ran up the ramp as fast as he could.

The ragged group of men were not ones to accept defeat. They charged out of the trapdoor and started chasing the two. Roni struck a couple in the head with the zoon as they emerged.

The first two fell back unconscious on top of the ones trying to scramble out. The whole lot fell into a heap at the bottom of the cavern. Slowly, they got up and made their way out. By the time, the men had some kind of order, Roni and Eyvind were some distance away, running as fast as they could in the southeast direction, using the sun as their anchor in the sky. They were now concerned about the many trapdoors buried in the ground through which they could fall again into the hands of these primitive savages.

They looked behind to keep watch on the ruffians climbing out and chasing them, but there was no stopping Roni and Eyvind. This freedom had come with great difficulty, and they were not going to let anyone entrap them again. They pushed themselves yet harder to gain distance from their pursuers, whose yells could be heard over the expanse.

Roni wished she had the ability to stop time as she had done before when she was in Imen-Hera. Alas, no longer possible. Eyvind looked over his shoulder frequently to keep a check on the men. With each stride of their feet, the two pushed their bodies harder to make their escape.

Roni was getting firsthand experience at being fully mortal with emotions surging in her of pain, fear, and strangest of all, the need to hurt someone in self-defense. This was most difficult for her to contend with. The Imen used their powers to heal, not hurt. This world was cruel and vicious, and she was caught in the quandary of regret for her actions, but at the same time, being around Eyvind dispelled this remorse.

The men behind them were relentless in their pursuit through the harsh Barren terrain. They threw knives at the two but fell short of striking them.

Far away, a forest emerged low on the horizon. Roni pointed to it as she ran breathlessly.

Eyvind screamed, "There it is! We can make it if we keep this distance from them."

He looked back to check, but what he noticed caused his heart to stop for a beat or two. The ominous whirling wind had returned, dancing across the surface at a higher speed and gaining on their pursuers.

"The Demon wind is back. We need to get to a tree fast," he yelled out to Roni.

She couldn't believe it. They couldn't seem to catch a break. From the moment she had left Imen-Hera, she had been on the run continuously, managing to escape one horrific experience after another. Just when she thought the worst was over, there was always something bigger and more dangerous looming over them.

Will we ever reach the White Forest? What else awaits us now?

These thoughts kept tormenting her as she pumped her legs faster, turning her neck to have a look. The men were chasing them, and the Demon wind was chasing all of them. It was hard to ascertain if the men were aware of the whirling funnel because they paid it no heed and were riveted on their targets.

Eyvind looked at the knobby trees they passed by, knowing they couldn't stop to access, as they were still being chased. This worried them both.

He turned his head and saw the winds getting closer. "The men are still chasing us. The Demon is getting closer. No telling who will catch us first. I think it'll be the wind. We need to find a tree to cling on to; or else, we won't make it."

Lust and greed had seized the skeletal louts, and they were willing to take bigger risks just for the opportunity to capture Roni and the bobble on her finger. They continued to doggedly pursue them even as the devil wind whipped from right to left and began to gain on the scrawny men.

The sky grew dark, and the air was once again electrified. Now all the humans felt the force of the malicious whirling gale tugging at them.

Eyvind looked over his shoulder and was mortified to see the man at the rear of the pack get plucked off the ground and carried away in the air, his screams lost in the roaring twister.

Roni pointed to a large, gnarled tree at a short distance.

The detritus of the land and the force of the wind made their progress impossible. It was just a matter of moments before they too would be whisked away into the dark, menacing mouth of the Demon and torn to bits.

With the air getting filled with dirt and debris and the skies darkening further, they were no longer able to look behind to assess their situation. They pushed hard in the direction of the tree Roni had spotted moments ago, but the wind tugged them backward. However much they tried, they seemed to be not moving at all.

Eyvind leaned low and holding Roni by her hips, pushed her forward with all his might. Behind, they could hear the muffled screams of the men as the Demon plucked them off one by one and carried them away to their doom.

"Can you see anything?" Eyvind asked.

"No!"

He pushed her as hard as he could, using all his strength, and she too leaned forward to add to his momentum. But they barely made any progress. Inch by inch, they moved across the tortured land, with Roni holding her arms outstretched in front of her, searching for the tree. Behind them, the roaring winds and muffled shrieks continued to be heard.

Are any of the men surviving?

The force of the wind had reached a zenith, and Eyvind feared lifting his foot off the ground, knowing they would be sucked into the gaping mouth of the raging Demon.

Just then, Roni stubbed her toe against a large root. "Here! It's here."

Eyvind pushed her to the ground, and they searched for the root. Large and twisted, it looked to be strong enough. They followed it right to the base of the tree. Neither of them was sure if this would work, but it was their only chance of survival. By now, the wind had started pulling at their clothes, and it was almost impossible to cling on to the tree trunk.

Eyvind tried to protect Roni with his body, shielding her from the pummeling strength of the wind and the pounding debris. He held her body down, and his arms and legs were wrapped around the thick root, with Roni secured underneath him.

As they clung to each other and to the giant root, Eyvind felt something grab his ankle. He craned his head and was horrified to see a bony hand clutching his foot in a death grip and slowly begin clawing up his body.

It was the leader of the savages. He was trying to push Eyvind off Roni while keeping a firm hold on his leg.

Eyvind struggled to find the dandum stick that was wedged beneath their bodies. He kicked at the leader with his other leg, hoping to pry him off. But he couldn't. He needed a weapon or even a free hand, but releasing his grip from the tree root would result in being carried off by the Demon itself, along with Roni.

Roni could feel Eyvind struggling with someone. She slowly half-turned and moved her head from underneath him. She saw the leader pounding Eyvind's back, hoping to shove him off her.

She too tried to find her zoon or the dandum, but in all the commotion, neither couldn't be located. She recalled all the items that had been given to her before her departure, and one of them was a dagger in a sheath. She wiggled her fingers to get to her left side where the blade lay pressed flat against her rib cage. An awkward and difficult position to reach while being pinned down, but she knew it was their last hope.

The bandit was persistent, hitting Eyvind repeatedly. Dust made him squint his eyes but couldn't shake off his determination to claim Roni as his prize. He had a tight hold of Eyvind's legs, and Roni couldn't shove him off Eyvind, given the position she was in.

She panicked when she saw the leader gaining the upper hand and clawing Eyvind's back. She knew it wouldn't be long before he managed to pry off Eyvind's grip around the tree root and send him flying into oblivion.

I have to do something.

She used all her might to reach for the dagger and tried to work it out of its sheath. But the harder she pulled on the dagger, the more her arm became trapped until it was completely immobile under both their bodies and the added weight of the leader. Also, there was an intense drive to hold on to the tree, lest the Demon wind accomplish its mission of shredding them to bits.

Roni felt an increasing pressure pushing her down further, and as she wrenched her head to look, she saw the leader violently trying to pry Eyvind's arm off. He even bit his back and shoulder to get him to release his grip, but Eyvind quietly bore it all and fought back, regardless of the pain.

Fear struck Roni like lightning at the thought of losing Eyvind, bringing with it an inferno of rage. This gave her the strength she needed, and with a mighty pull, she freed the hand that held the dagger by its hilt. She tried to stab at the leader, but being at an awkward angle, she had no range or flexibility to harm him.

She tried to open her eyes to see where the man was before she took the chance to strike again, but all her attempts were in vain. She was unable to reach any vital areas. The leader was still clawing at Eyvind's body and had almost overpowered him. This caused Roni to twist her arm and with one hard jab, she struck the leader in the leg, barely missing Eyvind. She could feel the blade penetrate his flesh and strike the bone.

"Arghh…!" A cry of pain and the leader released his hold on Eyvind and instinctively reached for the blade that was embedded in the side of his calf. Roni held on to the blade as the howling leader reached for it and tried to get it off his calf.

This maneuver gave Eyvind the breathing space from the constant pummeling to think and find a way to protect them. He scanned the area around their bodies for anything that could be used as a weapon. He found a big rock stuck between the root and the ground.

With a calming breath to settle his nerves, he held Roni tightly to his chest with one hand and gripped the rock with the other. Twisting his upper body, he struck the marauder in his chest with all the strength he could muster, the only place he could hit him.

This force was enough to knock the wind out of the leader, causing him to instinctively arch up to gasp for a breath. That gave the

Demon wind the opportunity to pry him off Eyvind. It worked.

The leader's bony fingers tried to grab onto anything anchored to the ground, including Eyvind, but he was unable to overcome the vicious force that finally carried him off into oblivion.

Eyvind and Roni breathed out a sigh of relief, but their problems were far from over. They still had to fight to survive the cyclone. They clung tightly to the thick root and to each other.

The devilish wind blew in circles and tried to wrench them away, but the stronger it tried, the harder they gripped. They wanted to survive this ordeal at any cost.

At long last, the wind surrendered and moved along.

Eyvind and Roni stayed clinging to one another as well as to the root well after the Demon had passed.

When all was still and the dust had settled down a bit, they emerged from the thick layer of dirt that had encapsulated them. They were exhausted and drained of their energy. Rising to their feet, they looked around to see if any signs of the ruffians remained. The land was motionless and silent once again.

The cyclone had carried away all signs of life, save the trees.

They looked at one another, and neither could recognize the other. They looked like the strange dark creatures that had emerged from the ground.

Roni couldn't help but laugh at Eyvind, and he joined in. There was nothing humorous about their situation, but it was the only thing they could do to release the tension of what they had been through.

Roni began to dust herself off, but Eyvind stopped her with a gesture. "Wait. Don't dust off. Stay covered in dirt until we reach the White Forest. It will play to our advantage in case someone is spying on us through the trapdoors. We look no different than the filthy thugs who live in the caverns below. We'll come across as one of them from a distance."

Roni nodded and smiled at his brilliant idea. They hurried as fast as they could in the direction of the distant forest. As they got closer, a surge of energy invigorated them, propelling them to run faster.

"Why do those men live in such harsh conditions, enduring starvation and the terrible wind when they could have easily moved to the forest or elsewhere?"

Eyvind had no reply to her question. They ran in silence.

It wasn't long before they reached the edge of the forest, but this time, they were cautious. Before entering, they looked up at the canopy. It certainly was a white forest.

The trees bore white barks, and all the fresh leaves were almost devoid of color with the mature leaves having a pale green pigment. These were the strangest trees both had ever seen.

They looked into the forest to see if anything stirred but detected no signs of life. Nevertheless, they had the strange sensation they were being watched by hidden eyes.

"I wonder what awaits us in here," commented Roni.

"Yes. I wonder the same," replied Eyvind. "Let's find out."

They searched for a path, but there seemed none. It felt as if no one had traveled in or out of the forest for a long time. They looked back at the forsaken land of furious winds behind them. They couldn't return there. So, they entered, regardless of the solitude. Now, there was no turning back.

They made their way cautiously into the forest, and as they moved deeper with each stride, they noticed the vegetation becoming denser and more difficult to navigate. They kept a watchful eye for the impending danger or any sign of life. They found none, though they could feel invisible eyes on them.

Eventually, they heard the chirping of birds and other little creatures, but there was still no sight or sound of people. In fact, the ground bore no tracks of anyone having lived there either.

Eyvind's training took over, and he began to scour the ground, looking for any signs of life other than animals.

"This is strange. I can't find tracks of anyone other than animals. Are you sure this is the right place?" he asked.

"I'm certain of it," she replied.

Roni then looked around and began to doubt herself. She wondered if she had made a mistake, but the more she thought about it, the more certain she became that this was indeed *the* place. She clearly remembered her parents telling her about this forest.

"This *has* to be it," she muttered as she looked up at the trees and all around. There were no signs of anyone having been there in a long time. Cautiously, they made their way deeper into the forest and prepared themselves mentally for their next challenge.

WHEN RAIDON WOKE UP in the morning and emerged through the thicket barrier, he was shocked at the sight that met him.

A strange, tortured land.

He wondered what entity had cursed such a forsaken place. As a soldier who was used to seeing lush woods and vegetation in Carron, he found the desolate landscape alien with its twisted trees stripped of foliage, along with strange boulders jutting out from the ground. And no other signs of life: no roads, trails, or markers of habitation.

He looked at the ground to see if he could find Roni's or Eyvind's tracks.

I wonder if they have made it so far. But they must have, as both are strong and determined.

His instincts fueled his thoughts as he frantically searched for their tracks, walking back and forth along the ridge of the cliff when he finally came across some signs. Tracks of Eyvind's shoes and smaller footprints of Roni's.

His relief was palpable, and he was determined to find them. Before following Eyvind's tracks, he went back to the thicket and peeked over the edge of the mountain range to see if any soldiers were scaling their way up. He saw at least 10 bodies laid out at the base of the mountain, the ones who had perished while attempting to ascend the night before and about half a dozen soldiers stirring about.

He didn't want to take any chances, so he quickly made his departure and began to follow the tracks across the Barren wasteland.

The strange stillness of the deserted landscape put him on edge. It was as though he was being watched by an invisible entity. He didn't like that eerie feeling and became alarmed with each step he took forward.

Only the fact that he was following Eyvind's and Roni's footsteps gave him the confidence to keep going. He picked up his pace, especially when the prickling feeling of invisible eyes on his back grew intense.

He looked around hoping to catch a glimpse of any shadow following him, but there was nothing in all directions. It was too strange. He started running across the terrain, hunting the ground for tracks, until they suddenly vanished. Examining the ground carefully, he found no signs of foul play, but he also couldn't make out where Eyvind and Roni had disappeared.

"The wind must have erased their prints. I'll just keep going in the southeast direction. I may find them again," he muttered to himself, scratching his head. He ran some distance, occasionally flitting his eyes to the ground for some indication about Roni and Eyvind.

As he hurried along, the ominous feeling that had been haunting him since he set foot in this place increased in intensity. It began gnawing at his insides, and alarms rang in his head. Raidon ran as fast as he could until he saw an open trapdoor ahead and a strange skeletal creature climbing out of it.

"So, it's you who has been watching me!" he exclaimed to himself. He could not tell at this point if he was friend or foe. Three more withered men climbed out and stood facing him. He wondered if Eyvind and Roni had been accosted by them and hence, there were no footprints.

He stared at the men, and they kept a watchful eye on him. A standoff ensued for a breath or two until one of them let out a loud cry followed by another high-pitched scream from someone behind Raidon at a short distance. He looked back and saw four more emaciated men charging toward him.

Raidon sidestepped them and ran as fast as he could. He wondered how many trapdoors existed in this strange Barren wasteland. He zig-zagged left to right as they came at him with force and vengeance.

He rushed to the left when he saw three more coming toward him from the right. They kept chasing him relentlessly. Cursing for the lack of weapons to defend himself with, he knew speed was his only ally.

He pushed the two standing in front of him and dodged the other three. The men threw daggers at him, but luckily, they missed each time. One of them landed on the ground in front of him, and he was tempted to pick the weapon up, but he didn't have the second it would take to do so. His attackers were closing in on him.

He thought he could outrun them when he saw several trapdoors opening in the distance with similar gaunt men climbing out of them. He was outnumbered. They were coming for him from every direction. Looking at them popping up from the ground, he became worried for his life. He could hardly believe the scene in front of him. This was the third time he was facing death in so many days.

Have these creatures captured Eyvind and Roni? He had no time to think of any other thoughts when he found himself completely surrounded by the withered men.

He slowed his pace and then came to a halt. There was no place to run. There were too many of them, and they had closed in on him from all sides. He turned around to find a route of escape, but the men were tightly packed as more emerged from the ground. He had nowhere to go and no weapons to fight with. They held crude daggers in their bony hands with the tips pointed at him. Raidon was sure he was going to die.

THE VEGETATION GREW INCREASINGLY dense as they moved deeper into the forest. Eyvind and Roni didn't speak much but remained alert the entire time, not knowing what to expect. The feeling of being watched never left them. After covering some distance, when nothing attacked them, they decided to stop and rest for a while.

Roni gravitated toward a large tree that reminded her of the Boad tree and sat beneath it. Eyvind joined her. They rested quietly, each lost in their own thoughts. This was the first chance they had to think about what they had left behind.

Eyvind had no regrets about his decision whatsoever, but the only thing that was scraping his guts was the concern he had for his mother. He knew she would never believe the story his father would spin and would challenge him, which might irk the King. But there was nothing he could do from here.

Roni wondered how her parents were and if Suki and Kenji were missing her as much as she was missing them.

Eyvind and Roni knew they were embarking on a new beginning, and they resolved to take on any challenge thrown their way without hesitation. But at the moment, they were so exhausted and absorbed in their thoughts that they were unaware of the beings who had materialized from nowhere and were standing behind them.

Stealthily, without a sound, they glided forward until they stood alongside the two. The sentinels of the forest. The giant white wolves that blended perfectly with the terrain.

"You must be from Imen-Hera because only they can make it this far," spoke a gentle voice, startling Eyvind and Roni.

They jumped to their feet and turned around quickly, ready to defend themselves. Before them stood three men and a woman and two giant white wolves. Roni and Eyvind were unaware of the numerous other wolves that remained camouflaged in the trees and the surrounding foliage.

"Who are you?" asked Roni.

"We asked you first. You are from Imen-Hera, are you not?" said one of the men. He was thin, older, and soft-spoken, with a voice that was soothing and offered no threat.

Eyvind pulled Roni closer to protect her. He was uncertain whether they were friend or foe. Thus far, in their journey, they had met only foes. Though the man's calm tone indicated no harm or malice, he did not want to take a chance, especially after what they had been through.

The other two men were shorter and thinner than the first and considerably younger, resembling Kenji in appearance with their dark hair and similar facial features. The woman was slightly older but thin and beautiful with high cheekbones and flawless skin. Her eyes exuded wisdom, and Roni was reminded of her own mother. Her air of quiet confidence made Eyvind long to see his mother. As moments passed, the air surrounding them became less tense.

"I *am* from Imen-Hera, banished from there," Roni admitted embarrassingly, causing the rest to throw sympathetic glances at her. She cast her eyes down and waited for the Elders to castigate her.

"There is nothing to be ashamed of. We too have knowingly made decisions in the pursuit of different destinations and desires. That is why we're here. Welcome," the woman consoled Roni.

The others set their curious glances on Eyvind. From his features, it was obvious he was not an Imen. Tall and well-built, he was a true soldier and looked much different than the others, even though both of them were heavily covered in dirt and resembled creatures from another world.

Eyvind stepped back, allowing Roni to interact with them. His duty was done as he had successfully delivered her to her new home. He was the odd man out and wondered where he should go from there. Wanting to be with Roni and knowing he had unfinished tasks to be undertaken in Carron, his awkwardness increased.

Raidon too had not made an appearance here to help him in this decision. He didn't even know if his friend had made it to the Talbot

Mountain range. There was also an important task of disinterring Axel's body from the suffocating grave and releasing his spirit into the afterlife. Besides, his home was Carron, not the Carron he left behind, sculpted by his father, but the one he had envisioned. A different kingdom where people shared the values of a forgotten time. He wondered what the future held for him.

Though he was drawn to Roni and didn't want to leave her, he felt unwelcome amongst the others.

"I am Kirio, the Elder," introduced the woman.

"And I am Shuzuko, the Elder," stated the older man.

"I am Doru," said the third.

"Foruki," introduced the fourth as he looked at Eyvind, who was lost in his own thoughts, with great suspicion. When he came to, he was a little embarrassed at being caught not paying attention. His mind was on his mother. He worried about her intensely and felt something bad had happened to her.

"And who are you?" asked Kirio in a kind tone.

"I'm Eyvind. Eyvind from Carron," he replied in the same manner.

"Carron?" asked Kirio and Shuzuko. They wondered why he had accompanied an Imen.

Foruki, who was suspicious of everything, became alarmed. His body stiffened, and his jaw clenched. He trusted no outsiders.

Roni became aware of his sudden stiff posture and intervened. "Eyvind rescued me and ensured my safety until I reached here," she explained.

"What would prompt a stranger, *especially* one from Carron, to help one of us?" Foruki asked in a highly distrustful tone.

Eyvind was not expecting this kind of reception or the pitch of the accusations. He opened his mouth to answer but changed his mind out of respect for Roni. The rest awaited an answer, but he felt uncomfortable giving it to them. This was Roni's story to tell.

The giant canine beasts standing beside them sensed the tension and grew uneasy, shuffling their feet on the ground. Kirio motioned them to settle down.

Roni was visibly affronted and jumped to his defense. "It's true. *I* was banished from

Imen-Hera for *my* wrongdoing. Eyvind chose to leave his home and become a fugitive for *my* sake," she explained without giving too many details.

"A fugitive? Are we to expect an army to come chasing after him? And why is he a fugitive in the first place?" asked Foruki in great concern.

"Foruki. Please! This is no way to welcome them," rebuked Shuzuko.

"But with all due respect, he *is* a threat to us. He's an outsider. We cannot allow him into our sanctum. Especially a fugitive," he retorted.

"Please! He's no threat to you," pleaded Roni.

Shuzuko and Kirio came to a tacit decision to allow Eyvind to accompany them and be questioned later. If he did pose a threat, they would let the guardians deal with him.

The guardians patrolled the forest and kept everyone out, especially those who entered with malice in their hearts. This was another reason why the guardians had not attacked Eyvind, which reassured Shuzuko and Kirio. However, Foruki was still dissatisfied.

"Come. Let's offer them our hospitality," said Kirio, beckoning them in her direction.

Everyone, except for Foruki, followed Kirio's lead. Foruki remained behind and stared in the direction from where Eyvind and Roni had come. His paranoia consumed him.

He scrutinized the area to see if they had brought other unwelcome guests with them. He called for the wolves and motioned them to patrol the forest and keep a vigil for any strangers. Foruki remained for a while and eventually followed the rest.

Roni and Eyvind were led through the thick vegetation until they arrived at an area where a dense population of giant trees grew amongst the smaller ones with the white bark.

Kirio and Shuzuko stopped to face their guests.

"Welcome to Bal-Shera," she said.

Eyvind and Roni looked around, but there was nothing except the forest. They saw no signs of habitation. It seemed odd.

Kirio was aware of their confusion. She smiled and pointed at an enormous tree. A doorway opened in the massive giant's belly of a trunk, and a carved stairway was revealed.

The mammoth tree pierced through the dense canopy of the smaller trees, thereby shielding its actual size from those at the bottom.

Roni was amazed! It reminded her of Imen-Hera.

They were ushered into the belly of the tree and began their ascent. The tree center was hollow with its nurturing veins running through the thick outer ring. It was a steep ascent.

The expression on Foruki's face expressed displeasure in letting Eyvind into their sanctuary. He marched up the rear until they reached Bal-Shera, the city in the sky.

It was spectacular. The city was built upon hundreds of treetops sitting high in the clouds. All the structures were white and airy, with the entire place giving the appearance of being bright and beautiful. Hundreds of delicate filigree bridges connected the different structures and buildings together. They were like an intricate web of interwoven fine metalwork that had been curved and twisted to create unique patterns.

Exquisite! That was the first thought that hit Roni as she took in a deep breath. The air was crisp and thin, but it felt wonderful after the dust and debris that had hit them by the Demon wind. The Bal-Sherans had adapted to the entire environment.

Roni and Eyvind ambled through the city along with their group of four, looking frightening in their dirt-enveloped states. The others stared at them in horror as they passed by. There were questions on everyone's faces about who and from where the strangers came from, and how they had managed to come there.

The group eventually arrived at an enormous hall that had a panorama of elongated windows all around, allowing light to filter in. The Imperial Hall of the Elders. Their main assembly room.

At one end of the hall, Roni and Eyvind saw a group of Elders sitting upon oversized ice-blue-and-silver winged chairs, with stern expressions on their faces. Kirio and Shuzuko took their places at the empty seats.

Roni and Eyvind were introduced to the rest of the council as they approached and stood before them.

There were five of them, two women and three men, including Kirio and Shuzuko, all thin and about the same stature.

One of the women spoke, "Welcome to Bal-Shera. We've been told one of you is an Imen and the other is from Carron."

"That is true," Roni said, and Eyvind nodded.

"We have also been informed that you're a fugitive," commented another Elder, addressing Eyvind.

"That's also true," replied Eyvind with respect.

"May I ask why?" the woman asked, leaning forward to hear his reply.

Eyvind hesitated, feeling awkward answering the question because he was aware it would lead to more questions and disbelief. He thought about his answer for a brief moment and then chose to tell them the truth as boldly as he could.

"Because I renounced my claim to the throne," he began in a matter-of-fact manner.

Laughter broke out from a few observers in attendance.

"Please!" yelled out Shuzuko in a stern manner, addressing those who were laughing.

Silence was restored immediately.

Gyesho, another Elder, leaned forward to probe Eyvind's statement further.

"You're an heir to the throne of *Carron*? Is that what you're telling us?" he asked in complete disbelief.

"I *was* the heir to the throne," Eyvind corrected him.

"What drove you to renounce your throne, young man?" Gyesho continued.

Eyvind was put on the spot. He had never stopped to face the true reason why he *had* made this decision. He glanced at Roni, who was staring down at the floor motionless, suffering through her own guilt and embarrassment.

"Well?" asked Gyesho again, now leaning forward even more in anticipation of Eyvind's answer.

"Principles and love. That's what drove me to this decision, and I refused to abide by my father's wishes," he stated boldly as he looked at Roni. He could hardly believe the words that had come out of his mouth.

Stunned by his admission, Roni looked up at him.

The uneasy tension that had existed in the back of his mind suddenly vanished. For once, he felt at ease around her. The truth had set him free and allowed his heart to revel in the beauty of his emotions.

Roni blushed underneath all the dirt covering her face and was not sure how she should react to such an admission. She stood still with her hands folded in front of her.

A rustle of murmurs, expressing doubt and disbelief, went around among some members of the council.

"Strange."

"Absurd."

"Irrational."

Roni stepped forward to recount her whole story and tell them everything that had transpired since she first met Eyvind.

They were amazed to hear her tale, but even more so when they heard she was the daughter of Mihara and Kimiko, the Emperor and Empress of Imen-Hera. They rose from their chairs and approached her for a closer examination.

"It is she, whom the old have talked about," commented one of the Elders.

Roni was completely confused after hearing the statement.

They moved in closer, and Nouri, the other female Elder, approached Roni and wiped the dirt and dust off her face. She stepped back and looked at her quietly. The others stared at Roni with deep interest.

"The sacred text mentions she would arrive with two guardians," commented Nouri, as she stared at both of them and wondered where the third person was. "We only see one. Is there another with you?" she asked.

Eyvind took the liberty to answer. "Yes, there's another who was accompanying us, but he risked his life to help us get away. He's expected to reach here soon. That is if he wasn't captured while trying to aid our escape," Eyvind stated.

Nouri stared at him unaffected. "Is he also from Carron?" she asked.

"Yes, he's an Imperial Knight," replied Eyvind with pride.

"It will be difficult for him to reach here even if he makes it through the Barren. The guardians will not allow him passage," she replied calmly.

This alarmed both Eyvind and Roni. They became anxious.

"We can't leave him to die in the Barren or at the hands of the guardians. Those…those…creatures will kill him. We must go back to fetch Raidon," asserted Roni.

"No. I'll go back to look for him," declared Eyvind.

The Elders showed little concern for the missing companion and instead focused on Roni. "It will be prudent for you to remain here and let your friend go in search of him," stated Nouri.

Roni looked at Eyvind in grave concern, now worried for his safety. She knew he would not be permitted re-entry into the White Forest by himself and would be subjected to the guardians who kept watch. They would tear them to shreds.

"I'll go with him. You know very well he will not be permitted back. They have both risked their lives for me. Eyvind has even surrendered his right to the throne. I will not allow them to perish. After all, I'm indebted to them. It's not the way of the Imen," she pleaded emphatically.

"You're no longer an Imen," Kirio corrected her politely.

Roni wondered what they were going to do with Eyvind. She could not let him die at the hands of the savages in the Barren or by the white wolves. She had not expected such hostility toward him by the Elders. She made the resolve to remain with Eyvind no matter what, even if it meant being cast out.

"We came together, and we'll leave together. If you cannot guarantee his safety, then my decision remains firm. I mean no disrespect," she replied.

Eyvind was deeply touched by her stance. However, he would rather have sacrificed his life than subject her to more cruelty.

Before anyone could respond to her statement, Shuzuko spoke. "My dear, we're not cruel people, but we have our rules and laws. We mean no harm to this brave man. It's just the way things are. It's a fact the guardians will not allow him into the forest alone. He's not one of us.

"But first, let's examine and verify something far more important. We have to confirm if you are indeed the One the prophecy is written about. Either way, we cannot violate our ways of life and deliberately invite trouble or bend the rules and allow forbidden strangers to come and go as they please. It puts our very existence at risk. You must understand our position," he explained.

Roni knew it was futile trying to talk them into helping Eyvind. His fate was sealed. They did not want him in Bal-Shera. She wondered about the prophecy.

"What does the prophecy say about the chosen one?" she asked.

"The chosen one is our future Queen," Kirio replied.

Roni was shocked and pondered the words. *If that is true, I will just have to make it work in my favor. I won't leave Eyvind's side.*

Without saying anything further, she nodded in agreement to let them verify and agreed to come along with Shuzuko.

The Elders gathered around an elaborate podium upon which sat an ancient volume encased in glass.

One of the Elders opened the glass cautiously and removed the tome. He held it in the crook of his arm and turned the pages with great care. His thin finger dragged softly across the pages as he quietly read the text.

All eyes were upon him.

After a few moments, he looked up and said, "Ah, here it is." He pressed the tip of his finger on the page as he read along.

"The Queen of Bal-Shera shall be delivered by two guardians on the edge of winter. A ring with a stone as blue as the twilight sky full of twinkling bright stars shall adorn her finger. It is the worship stone akin to the one set in the crystal crown to adorn her."

Kirio rushed to Roni's side and took her left hand to search for the ring, but it was not there. Before she could grab the other hand, Roni held it up for her. The ring was encrusted with dirt.

Kirio wiped the layer of dirt to reveal the sparkling stone. It was exactly as described. Her eyes grew big as she drew in a deep breath and held Roni's hand up so the rest could see.

They were amazed. They bowed before her and remained bowing until Roni waved her hand, releasing them from the posture.

Becoming queen was not something she had anticipated. She had just wanted a safe place for herself, Eyvind and Raidon.

"We have awaited you for generations. It's said that during your reign, we'll forever be changed as a nation and as a people. We are not certain what that means, but it's where the prophecy ends. Nothing more is written past that. To think this event is taking place in our lifetime… Wondrous," replied one of the Elders in excitement.

For a moment, everyone forgot about Eyvind.

During all this, as Roni awaited this confirmation, she found herself waning, reaching the point of near collapse from exhaustion. She mustered all her strength and stated her wishes. She had to do this for Eyvind.

"As Queen, would it not be your obligation to carry out my wishes?" she asked.

The Elders became silent and wondered what she was about to ask of them.

"Yes, it would," answered Nouri apprehensively. They were not accustomed to taking orders from anyone, because until now they were the authority over Bal-Shera, and their word was final. Now they would have to acquiesce to Roni's orders.

"Good. Then as the Queen, I make a humble request to send Eyvind out to the Barren with *aid* and bring back our other companion. If it's written in this ancient book that I would be accompanied by two, then it's *your* duty to make sure they're accepted and treated as equals," she stated with authority.

There was silence all around. No one said a word.

"Does the text mention banishing them after delivering me here? Does it?" she continued.

They were cornered and had no answer in their defense. They had no choice but to comply with her wishes. Furthermore, she was right, there was no mention of harming the companions.

Roni started to sway, and Eyvind noticed it immediately. He grabbed her just as she began to crumple to the floor.

"She needs food, water, and rest!" He stated with alarm.

Everyone sprang into action, and Roni was carried away by several people and waited on.

The attention now shifted to Eyvind. Their demeanor toward him had changed. They reluctantly accepted him. It was the order of the Queen.

"You must also be tired and hungry. Follow him and he'll show you to your quarters. We hope to see you at the dinner feast," stated Shuzuko respectfully.

"No, I need to leave immediately to find my fellow companion," he replied anxiously.

"There's no need to be in such haste. First, get some food and rest. Meanwhile, we'll put together a party to go with you to find him," assured Shuzuko.

Eyvind relaxed a little, knowing help was at hand, and the stifling feeling began to subside. He was led away by Doru, who showed a deep interest in him and respected his bravery.

Later, that evening, the great hall had been transformed to hold a feast, where everyone would assemble. The winged chairs had been removed, and there was a raised dais with a high table kept in its place. In front of it, were two long lines of tables facing each other.

There was excitement in the air as the people of Bal-Shera had been alerted their Queen had finally arrived to claim the throne. They could hardly believe they were witnessing the ancient prophecy coming true.

Both Roni and Eyvind had been taken to their respective rooms and well cared for by the people of Bal-Shera. At long last, they could soak in hot water and get rid of the evidence of their days of hard travel. Both were given plenty to eat and drink and a soft bed to rest their weary bones. Then they had to get ready for the feast. Roni's coronation would take place over the next few days, but first, she had to be presented to the people of the White Forest.

Roni was dressed in a traditional long dark blue gown with tiny jewels stitched on it that sparkled in the light. On her feet, she wore soft white leather boots embellished with gems in a smooth scrolling pattern. A sparkling white band that pulled back her thick dark hair completed the look. She was amazed when she looked at herself in the mirror. She had been completely transformed from a dust-encrusted drab warrior to an elegant and feminine beauty.

All the important Bal-Sherans were present at the feast hall, including Eyvind. He exuded royalty, handsomely dressed in a long green tunic with wide overlapping front flaps that was adorned with a double row of ornate silver buttons, along with white pants and knee-high white boots. He sat tall and straight at his table, his countenance smooth, but he was plagued by a weird sense of anxiety.

Doru sat next to him, vying for his attention, as did many others. Eyvind wanted to leave right away to go in search of Raidon, but he had been unsuccessful at persuading the Elders. They insisted on his joining in the festivities as a support to Roni before granting him leave.

Soon the Elders arrived and took their places on the high dais. They were taken aback by Eyvind's appearance, looking so princely and royal. No one had seen a Carronite before, and Eyvind caught everyone's attention with his tall stature, golden hair, and blue eyes. He was different and exotic as compared to the Bal-Sherans.

Everyone awaited their Queen's arrival. Roni was nervous as she'd never imagined herself in such a situation. She knew nothing about being a Queen and ruling a nation and its people. And being the Queen of a strange land frightened her more. It seemed that with each turn, life was becoming more complex than she had ever anticipated. She yearned for her simple existence in Imen-Hera.

She took a deep breath to calm her nerves and focus on the present. She was here now and would have to deal with the tribulations she had brought upon herself. The thought of failure and not living up to everyone's expectations concerned her.

She thought about consulting Eyvind, but he knew nothing about these people or this land. It was now all down to her. She would have to use the knowledge she'd learned from her father and live up to the promises she had made to him.

Moments later, as she was standing just outside the great hall, she heard Shuzuko announcing to the people, "The One, the promised Queen who will lead Bal-Shera to a new chapter!"

Everyone rose and cheered Roni as she slowly made her way to her seat, and everyone gazed at her with great excitement. The people could hardly wait to find out what exciting chapter she would reveal and were looking forward to her message.

Roni looked regal and majestic. Eyvind's jaw fell open, and his heart pounded in a strange rhythm. He was stunned by her beauty and reverence. His mouth dried, and he had to swallow hard to speak. His eyes were trained on her the whole time.

From her seat in the center of the dais, her eyes too searched for Eyvind, but she couldn't find him in the sea of smiling faces.

Then everyone was called to attention by Shuzuko who continued with his announcement.

"You are invited here today to bear witness to a prophecy written in the Book of the Ancients: our most sacred text bearing our laws and ways, past and future. The prophecy of the arrival of our Queen has come to be. Our Queen has arrived."

The whole place cheered.

"My fellow Elders have attested and verified that she is indeed the One. She was delivered to us by two others, as written in the Ancient Text. One of her companions is here with us while the other, who helped them escape, is following behind. May I introduce Roni, who will be crowned Queen of Bal-Shera in three days."

Roni rose and bowed to the cheering crowd. She was instructed not to deliver a speech until her coronation. Shuzuko remained standing by her side and gestured for her to be seated.

"May I also introduce Eyvind of Carron, Roni's companion," he pointed to him.

Eyvind rose to his feet and bowed before a happily cheering assembly.

"Now we must celebrate this momentous occasion and feast well," Shuzuko yelled out.

Conversation and laughter filled the hall as everyone ate, drank, and spoke about Roni.

The Elders tried to engage her in their conversations, but her eyes kept searching for Eyvind amongst the enthusiastic banter and trilling laughter of the people. The Elders had forgotten about Eyvind and had seated him quite far from the dais.

She was affronted by the fact they had considered him merely as a companion who had safely brought her to them and whose status meant little here. Roni gave amicable answers to the questions thrown at her and engaged in polite conversation until she could no longer ignore the anxiety that came with the knowledge that the Elders had insulted the royal Prince.

She turned to them and asked, "May I ask why Eyvind was not seated more prominently?"

The Elders were surprised by her concern.

"There's nothing to worry about. He's seated with the best and is being taken care of well. We mean no disrespect," stated Nouri.

Roni became annoyed by her irreverence and tried to restrain herself. Her words were clipped as they were uttered to all the Elders. "He's not just a mere companion. He's the Prince of Carron. Royalty!"

There was silence at the table.

She requested a private council with them immediately. They rose from their seats and filed out of the great hall, apprehension visible in their body movements, while the others were told to continue with the feast.

Eyvind wondered what was going on. He couldn't tell much from the stoic expressions on all their faces. He was frantically worried about Raidon and wanted to get Roni alone to press the issue of sending out a search party for him at once.

However, something else was also bothering him, which seemed to compete for far more of his attention. A strange gnawing sensation was gripping his gut, making him feel as though something was being cleaved from within. His thoughts led him again to his mother. Little did he know that his mother had passed into the afterlife at that precise moment.

Roni and the Elders assembled in a small chamber where she proceeded to tell them in depth about all the feats Eyvind and his men had undertaken to get her to Bal-Shera in one piece. Riddled with anxiety for his safety, she then turned the topic to Raidon.

"I demand you gather a search party to find and bring back our other companion." She folded her arms across her chest, not ready to take no for an answer.

The Elders were perturbed by her request. "My Queen, we have never ventured out of the forest. It's forbidden."

Roni was shocked at their admission.

"Then I order you to find a group of able men or soldiers and send them out."

They remained befuddled and looked at one another.

Roni became frustrated by their inaction and decided to take matters into her own hands. "If you won't help, then I'll go with Eyvind to fetch Raidon."

She started for the door but was stopped by Shuzuko.

"We cannot allow you to leave on such a dangerous trek," he pleaded.

"You leave me no choice," she replied in frustration. "You don't understand. These men gave up everything and took risks with their lives for my safe arrival. It's the least I can do for them."

The Elders were at a loss for words. Roni's request was dangerous and forbidden, especially since they had already introduced her to the people. Although she had not been officially crowned, she was nevertheless their Queen.

They were left with no other choice but to comply with her orders. The problem lay in finding volunteers willing to venture beyond the forest. They came up with a resolution to allow Eyvind to go with a few wolves.

Roni agreed reluctantly.

Eyvind was summoned from the festivities and informed of the plan.

Roni again offered to go with him, but the council forbade her. She was aware Eyvind would need more than just himself to safely find and return with Raidon.

Meanwhile, Doru had also stolen away from the feast hall, trailing Eyvind, and had his ear pressed against the door, eavesdropping on their conversation. He wanted to go with Eyvind and could hardly contain himself standing on the other side.

Opening the door, Doru burst in. "I'll go with him!"

The council members were shocked at his intrusion and grit.

Roni was relieved at the volunteer's willingness to accompany Eyvind.

"I can get others to come along," he added in excitement.

The Elders were surprised at his admission.

Doru sprang into action and wanted to know when they would leave.

The nagging feeling clawing his insides, concerning his mother, continued to bother Eyvind. But that was beyond his control.So, he tried to keep his focus and tend to things that he *could* control.

"We need to find Raidon. He will not be able to make it across the Barren by himself," stated Roni with urgency, looking at Eyvind.

"I'll leave immediately." Eyvind was raring to search for his friend.

The Elders gave in to Roni's wishes and instructed the guard to allow seven wolves to go with Eyvind, Doru, and any others who wanted to accompany them at first light the next day.

Roni was pleased by the arrangements and felt tremendous relief at being successful in her first duty as a Queen. Eyvind and Raidon were important to her, and she would not let them down.

Early next morning, a small volunteer army of thirteen men, clad in leather (including Eyvind), assembled alongside seven wolves, who were readied to leave in haste. Each wolf was double-saddled to carry two riders. The wolves snarled at the air impatiently, eager to sink their canines into the enemy.

Equipped with javelins and zoons, this group rode through the forest in the direction of the desolate Barren of Bellwin.

As they quickly galloped on, it was not long before the forest started to become less populated with trees, indicating they were close to the edge. As the vegetation grew sparser, Eyvind could see the vast Barren on the horizon. The land was as tortured as before, but this time, he could feel Raidon was in trouble. He pushed his wolf harder and emerged out from the shelter of the forest and rode through the wasteland. Feeling the vibe of danger in the air, the wolves charged ahead in fury. Eyvind kept a keen eye out for the Demon wind as he knew others had no experience in dealing with the swirling gale.

They rode further into the cursed land when Eyvind saw some men gathered at a distance. He gestured to the Bal-Sherans and the wolves to follow him quickly and headed straight for them, instructing the wolves to charge in their direction. Foaming at the mouth, the canine beasts pushed forth with all their might.

Seeing them approach, the gaunt men scrambled to open a hatch in the ground and hurried in, forcibly shoving someone into the tunnels. Eyvind could tell it was Raidon from his build and stature as compared to the bony villains. He was relieved to know his friend was still alive and had made it thus far. With an energized cry, he charged ahead of the rest, wanting to get to the door before they closed it.

Eyvind and Doru jumped off and raced for the trapdoor as the giant wolf lunged at the skeletal attackers, throwing them to the ground. The ruffians hurried to close the hatch, but Eyvind jammed his javelin into the opening and pried it open before it could be bolted shut. After all, his previous experience had taught him how to deal with these louts.

The gaunt bandits ran through the tunnels, fearing the strange men as well as the huge beasts. Normally, they were relentless and brave, but this attack surprised them and sent them scattering through the narrow tunnels to gather their accomplices. They needed to be high in number if they hoped to survive Eyvind and his men.

Had it not been for the giant wolves, the marauders would have stood their ground and fought the Bal-Sherans on the Barren land. But with the inclusion of the wolves, they determined they could better defeat the attacking enemy within their tunnels.

Eyvind jumped down the open hatch and chased the ruffians. Doru and the others followed him, running through the network of underground caverns following the voices.

Closing the distance between them, Eyvind leaped in the air and thrust his javelin deep into the back of one of them, nearly piercing him through and through. The gaunt man fell to the ground with blood gurgling from his mouth as he lay gasping.

This time, Eyvind was deadly serious. He was attacking to kill. He jumped over the dying man while retrieving his weapon and continued running. Most of the Bal-Sherans followed him, but a few bypassed him and chased the band of misfits before they disappeared and used the darkness in the tunnels to their advantage.

Eyvind could hear the sounds of a struggle somewhere in front of him, but the dim light made it difficult to assess what was going on. He raced ahead and arrived at the scene of the scuffle along with his men and discovered bodies fighting. Arms thrashed, fists pounded, weapons clashed. Screams reverberated in the air surrounding them, along with the slashing sounds of metal blades hitting the rock walls.

Amid all this noise, one voice penetrated through the chaos directly into Eyvind's ears for the first time in a long while. Raidon.

"Eyvind! Is that you, Sire?"

"Raidon! We've come for you!" Eyvind roared.

"Then let's fight our way out!" Raidon shouted back with confidence.

Raidon and Eyvind now fought the ruffians together in perfectly choreographed moves. More cries were heard as the blades clanged and slashed, maiming everyone who stood in their way.

By now, most of the wolves had followed the Bal-Sherans into the tunnels, gnawing and tearing through the flesh of any marauders who fell in their way. Some of them stood guard at the trapdoor opening to prevent its closure or allow any of the louts to escape.

The fighting continued for a while as scrawny misfits arrived to defend their men, but between the gigantic wolves and Eyvind's men, they stood no chance. The news of this fight had traveled far and wide, causing more ruffians to keep pouring through the tunnels. Eyvind knew their own resources were limited, and they were soon reaching the point of exhaustion. Also, he didn't want more of the Bal-Sherans injured. This was not their fight.

He signaled to Raidon to start withdrawing and make his way back to the hatch.

They managed to push the ruffians away and made the wolves stand between them. Then Eyvind turned to his men and yelled, "Retreat! Back to the hatch!"

The group started moving backward while fighting and killing those who attacked them until they reached the trapdoor. The wounded were pulled out along with the wolves who watched their rear.

Doru did a quick head count to make sure no one was left behind in the tunnels. After everyone had made it to safety, Eyvind and Raidon raced out of the hatch, and once on the Barren flats, the wolves all huddled together and herded their masters from danger, growling menacingly at any advancing ruffians.

Blood and dirt stained their white fur, while the muscles of their back stood taut, ready to attack. Some of them bled from stab wounds, but those didn't seem to faze them in the least. They were completely focused on their duty to protect their masters and return them safely home.

It was a sight to behold. Twelve Bal-Sherans and two Carronites mounted seven giant wolves and rode hard and fast toward their forest sanctuary.

Trapdoors opened at different places as skeletal creatures emerged from the ground and tried to take them down without realizing the wicked swirling winds had appeared once again dancing back and forth across the landscape.

Eyvind knew firsthand the wrath of the Demon and hurried the wolves to outrun it and reach the safety of the forest. When he looked back, he saw the churning winds whipping across the land, picking the skeletal creatures off one by one and carrying them to the dark abyss of its mouth where death lay in wait for them.

And then it was their turn. The Demon was determined to make them its prey, but Eyvind and his men pushed the wolves as hard as they could to reach the edge of the forest. Eyvind could hear the roar of the Demon in his ears as the whipping gusts tore at his clothes.

The wind was at their heels as they entered the forest. Faces tense and bodies bent low on the backs of the wolves; they tore through to safety.

I T WAS A SOMBER day in Jasper. The Queen's death was announced to the public.

The jubilant mood of the celebration of Eyvind's wedding and the union of the two nations came crashing down. The tragic news stunned them and dampened their enthusiasm. The citizens couldn't believe it.

They dressed in white garments to respect the dead Queen as funeral preparations were rapidly completed. A long procession of mourners wound their way up to the funerary mound, a sacred place where spirits were released so that they could make their way to their next journey.

The Carronite custom called for a funeral pyre to be built on the mound upon which the dead are laid. Later, the ashes are taken to the highest mountain peak and scattered in the air, especially in the case of the death of a dignitary, such as the Queen.

Korin and Audun wore the traditional white garments as did the others, while King Camden and Tara wore suitable light-colored clothes out of respect. Their faces were wiped clean of their expressions as they politely waited for the rituals to be carried out. Only Adina, clad in white, sobbed uncontrollably throughout.

Audun and Korin headed the procession in front of Beyla's sarcophagus, while other family members, dignitaries, and finally, the subjects of Carron who had come to attend the funeral followed the coffin.

Tara paid close attention to everything around her and made mental notes for future use. There was so much richness and culture in this land that she was envious of everything she laid her eyes upon. She followed the rituals closely and observed all the Prefects who were in the procession. There had to be someone who was a weak link in this land's armor. Her mind never rested, always on the prowl to find all of Carron's weaknesses before she departs.

Beyla had been wrapped in white linen with an ornate paper mask, painted with her image, placed on her face. She was unadorned in this last stage before she left the world simply because the Carronites believed that only things that could be reduced to ash along with the body could enter the afterlife and nothing else. Hence her body too was in a wooden coffin.

An embellished royal carriage carried the sarcophagus to the mound, followed by the procession. When they arrived at the site, it was gently placed upon the pyre made of rare and fragrant wood, and the High Priest commenced the services.

He chanted verses from ancient texts and poured exotic oils upon the stack. Once the various prayers and blessings were concluded, the priest handed King Audun and Prince Korin two lit torches and instructed them to light the pyre.

In a flash, the fire spread, and the blaze cocooned the sarcophagus in no time. As the flames danced toward the sky, Audun and Korin watched stoically. Adina wept uncontrollably, making Tara despise her even more. Camden rushed to embrace his daughter sympathetically, and that annoyed Tara to no end.

At long last, the raging blaze began to die out, and the attendees were escorted back to the castle, leaving the priest to conclude the honorary ritual by respectfully directing Beyla's spirit to move on to her next stage. The High Priest had the additional duty of collecting the ashes and preparing them for the mountain ceremony from where they would be released into the air and carried off by the wind to the heavens.

The guests began to move out, with their heads bowed low in respect. Except for one: Tara. Her gaze kept shifting from one to the other until it landed on Prefect Banyon. Tara instantly recognized that he was not born of nobility, but instead had clawed his way up to his status just as she had done.

Shuffling sideways, she positioned herself in his line of vision, showing off her best profile. The moment their eyes met, he bowed respectfully. She acknowledged him with a surreptitious nod as her body leaned slightly toward him. Her entire demeanor communicated her interest in him.

Prefect Banyon felt privileged that this honor was bestowed on him. His confidence ballooned as did his ego. He stepped forward and then realized where they were. He felt it would be inappropriate to approach her at this time and instead decided to wait until they returned to the castle.

Camden waited for Tara to join them as he continued to console a weeping Adina. She was the only one who was an emotional wreck. The girl wanted to be with Korin but was not allowed as per their customs.

Korin had almost forgotten about her, his mind focused on executing their plans as well as finding Eyvind before he ruined matters any further.

Later in the day, the subjects of Carron gathered outside the castle, their numbers increasing as hordes of common people poured out into the streets to hear the King's speech.

"Queen Beyla was a diamond amongst all. She may have left our world, but her name will live on in Carron. Her kindness and the generosity of her heart were an inspiration to all, and her righteous spirit was a blessing she conferred upon everyone. Now all we can do to honor her is to keep her in our hearts and follow in her path. She will be forever remembered and deeply missed. But her legacy will stay alive in her wishes for her son, Korin. Today, I take this opportunity to announce the last wish of Queen Beyla. Now Korin will be the future heir to the throne and the one who will wed Princess Adina."

This speech was met with stunned silence followed by a roar of frenzied discussions the next instant. All the people gathered wondered what had happened to Eyvind.

Audun raised his hand in a universal sign of silence, and the crowd quieted to hear the next words.

"Eyvind refused to accept Princess Adina in marriage and thereby forfeited his right to the throne. In doing so, he surrendered his allegiance to Carron, thus becoming a traitor. By the laws of the nation, he is now subject to a trial for his treason."

The King had only finished announcing the last words when the crowd's furor rose to deafening decibels, making even Audun and Korin nervous. They were aware that Eyvind was well-liked by the subjects of Carron, but it was today they understood just how much.

Everyone was shocked and dismayed by this revelation, shaking their heads in complete disbelief. Many went along with the story and added their own fabricated gossip, yet there were others who refused to believe any part of it.

Looking at the rising protests from below, Audun was worried about a fracture in the sections of his people regarding this news. However, there was nothing he could do about it now. The die had been cast. He had to get the Carthinians out of Carron before he could rally his people and prevent a chasm.

Behind Audun, the dignitaries had been gathered to hear his speech, including Camden and Tara. Prefect Banyon snaked his way through them and positioned himself as close to Tara as he could without drawing attention to himself.

Tara was aware of his presence on the other side of her and glanced at him surreptitiously when Camden was preoccupied with the speeches and ceremony. Prefect Banyon too acknowledged her subtle signs.

Tara eventually found herself face-to-face with him when everyone turned to depart. He firmed his shoulders and respectfully introduced himself to both Tara and Camden.

"Prefect Banyon at your service, Your Highnesses."

"Pleased to meet you, Prefect," replied Camden.

Tara nodded once but did not utter a word. She studied her future pawn from the corner of her eye and turned to depart, leaving Banyon behind, gazing at her. Halfway down the path, she looked at him over her shoulder and gave him an alluring smile while staring straight into his eyes. All of this happened within a fraction of a breath, but Banyon understood. Her smile and demeanor indicated an interest in a private audience.

Banyon was puzzled by her, yet at the same time, his ego overcame any sensible alarm that might have gone off in his head. Everyone retired to their chambers to rest before the feast honoring the departed queen commenced. All except Tara and by default, Camden.

Tara paced back and forth in their chamber in deep thought and couldn't wait for the opportunity to meet with the Prefect.

Camden's eyes followed his wife's pacing and sensed the unease in her disposition. "Tara? What are you up to?"

"Planning and plotting, my dear husband," she replied with insincerity.

"Planning Adina's wedding and plotting to spy?" he confirmed.

"Something like that. Did you see the reaction of Audun's subjects?" she commented in glee. "They're clearly divided. Divided! Do you know what that means, Camden? We need to move swiftly and take advantage of this split in his people. It always starts with a tiny fracture which turns into a split, then a rift, until it finally shatters into pieces!"

Camden was impressed with her observations and calculations. His wife was truly a great strategist.

"I don't want to waste much time, Camden. This is a perfect opportunity to attack and conquer while they're at their weakest. By the way, I wonder what the actual tale is regarding that boy. However, it's of no concern to us. We need to move right away."

Camden was always amazed by his wife's ambitious desires and the zeal with which she pursued them. Once a goal was established, she never wavered from its path until it was attained. She was right this time too. Then his fatherly instincts and concern for Adina rose to the surface. "What about Adina? And this marriage?"

"You are a fool, Camden! Have you not paid any attention? Korin has no real interest in her. You can tell from the way he's been distancing himself from her. Haven't you seen it?" she remarked in annoyance while thinking that if everything was left to Camden, nothing would ever get done.

Her arms were folded in front of her as she paced back and forth, staring into nowhere. The twin waves of rage and jealousy burned like an inferno within her gut.

"We can still lead them on about the marriage. We need time to gather vital information. I have a plan I'm working on, and for now, the wedding will proceed as decided. Whether Adina is wed by then or not is a non-issue. It has to be the opportune time, and it's all that matters to me. Her silly romance is of no concern to us," she stated heartlessly.

Camden was taken aback by the intensity of Tara's intentions and plotting. He faced a dichotomy: his daughter's happiness or the chance to attack and conquer Carron. He stared at the ground for a while and shook his head. Though it appeared to be a difficult decision to make as a father who loved his daughter, the chance of conquering Carron evaporated his concerns for Adina.

Tara was pleased with his choice.

Later in the evening, the feast was in full preparation, although the mood was glum, it being a funerary banquet. The guests assembled in the main hall, and each dignitary brought along a traditional token gift for the dead as an offering.

Tara couldn't believe her eyes at the sight before her. She was astonished by the range of luxurious gifts the attendees from far-off regions were offering. The more she saw the riches, the hotter the fire raged within her to conquer Carron. She wanted all this for herself. She couldn't tolerate the stark difference between her people and the Carronites.

Looking back, she was ashamed of how unrefined and primitive the Carthinians were in comparison. She needed to do something and do it fast.

The attendees conversed with all and reminisced about the Queen. In Beyla's honor, only her favorite foods were served. And everything was so scrumptious. Tara had to stop herself from asking for a second helping.

After the meal, everyone mingled for a while, and Tara set to work. She scanned the room in search of Prefect Banyon while trying to be as inconspicuous as she could. Finally, after working the room, she put herself in the perfect's position, and their eyes met. With a discreet gesture, she motioned him to meet her outside.

Banyon excused himself and meandered to the balcony.

Tara waited awhile and then navigated outside, accompanied by her two guards. Under the pretense of needing fresh air, she made her way to the grand balcony where she saw Prefect Banyon. She pretended not to see him and walked around for a moment.

Banyon could hardly believe the Queen of Carthinia had tacitly requested his attention. He stood proud and erect until she was in close distance, and with the confidence of a lion, he approached her. "Your Highness. The air is nice and crisp this evening."

"So it is," she replied.

"Our customs must seem strange to you," he continued.

"That's expected. We're just saddened by this sudden tragedy during *our* visit," she replied, testing the waters.

"Yes. It was a shock for everyone," he replied somberly.

The insipid conversation changed when she gestured her guard to be at ease and allow her privacy. They kept a watchful eye on her from a distance.

"Prefect Banyon…" she began.

"At your service, Your Highness."

"Of all the Prefects in attendance, you seem to stand out to me."

"I do?"

"You appear bright and ambitious." Tara's words stroked his ego.

Banyon could hardly believe her interest in him as well as her recognition of his strengths. He stood preening, delighted in this attention.

She realized then she had him. She knew his kind. They were easy to manipulate and mold. She just needed to confirm positively.

"I'm flattered, Your Highness. Without ambition, one cannot get past obstacles standing in the way of achieving the end goal," he preached in arrogance.

"And what's *your* end goal?" she asked, faking her fascination with him.

Banyon was full of pride and could hardly wait to share some of his opinions with someone of her stature. "My end goal? To achieve the highest position of prominence."

"And what would that be?" she asked with yet deeper interest. This time she didn't have to feign it. His answer would tell her if he was the right man for the task.

Banyon had never entertained that thought before and had only said it off the cuff to impress her. He pondered a brief moment, trying not to look unprepared for the question. "A minister someday, perhaps."

"*Just* a minister?" she asked in playful disappointment, shaking her head and giving him a teasing smile. "Usually, the highest position of prominence is that of a king."

He liked her playfulness and wondered where it would lead. He nodded while keeping his tone serious. "The position of a King is highly unlikely, Your Highness. Whereas a minister is more attainable."

Tara smiled at him flirtatiously. She used her vampish charm to test the waters of his desires. "So, a minister? I see," she stated in a questioning tone, soliciting a better answer.

"Yes. That's the highest achievement one can aspire to," he reiterated with equal playfulness.

He wondered what she was alluding to or had in mind and was impatient to find out. He waited with bated breath, hoping to get an answer, but she offered no immediate words.

This was all Tara's ploy to bait and slowly reel him in at her own time. She kept him guessing and in suspense. A game she loved to play. She walked around seductively for a moment and then planted the seed.

"You have the foresight and qualities to attain much more than that, Prefect. I can always spot a man who's driven by ambition and fears no obstacles or challenges standing in his path," she used her words to stroke his ego.

Banyon was beside himself. He could hardly believe his own ears. No one had shown such interest or been so "accurate" in evaluating his talents before. He was impressed beyond belief.

As a soldier, he knew how to read and estimate the strategy of his enemy. However, he had never come across a situation where he needed to worry about a woman's ploys. In Banyon's mind, Tara was simply interested in him and hence, was flirting with him. He had no clue he was just a disposable pawn in her ruthless game of power and control.

He did not know Tara would never allow another of her own background as an equal partner for obvious reasons. Banyon served as a means to an end and nothing else. He was disposable.

Tara had found the perfect fool to help achieve *her* end goal. His ambition was the key to fulfilling hers. Next was wielding the weapon of seduction upon him. It would take some time, but it would be worth its weight in gold.

Banyon sensed her aspiration, and his lascivious mind fantasized grand dreams of an exceedingly elevated status. His greed and hunger for power surged. He fancied himself as a rising star. Grandiose dreams started weaving through his mind.

Tara pumped them up further. "I'm certain your true value and efforts aren't recognized or appreciated by your colleagues and those whom you serve. They underestimate you. I admire your capacity to work in a place where the rulers undervalue you. I wouldn't have been able to." She gave a fake little shudder to underscore that sentiment. With these words, she was successful in planting seeds of resentment and dissent.

Arrogant and lacking humility, all the attention from Tara went to his head and made him more insufferable. But that's what made him perfect for her plan.

Tara ended the conversation with an invitation. "Why don't you come down for a casual visit to Carthinia as a gesture of 'goodwill' between the two nations and to continue our discussions? We would love to have you. I promise you will get a private tour of my nation, extremely *private*."

She hid the smirk that made her lips curve up, silently congratulating herself on succeeding in her task of befriending someone on the inside—one whom she could get to succumb to her spell and retrieve any information she desired.

A job well done, she was pleased with herself. "The perfect puppet!" Her mocking laughter followed her as she left the grand balcony.

And the evening of the funereal feast was concluded with the distribution of the gifts to the citizens.

The next day Tara, Camden, and Adina met with Audun and Korin, as well as the dignitaries from both sides to sign the peace pact as well as establish the time and day for the wedding. Both sides signed the meaningless accord. And then the arguments started.

Adina wanted to be wed in Carthinia; however, Korin and Audun insisted on Carron. Tara sided with her daughter and stipulated they be wed by Carthinian traditions.

Both sides had their motives for wanting the ceremony in their respective nation. Each presented reasons why the ceremony should take place in their own lands. Neither was willing to give in.

Adina sobbed out loud in frustration.

Korin dutifully moved toward her, feeling the need to console her in public, even though, personally, he found her behavior abhorrent and unbecoming.

Their heated argument was interrupted by Aurelius' arrival, surprising both Audun and Korin. Derrik had informed him of Beyla's death and filled him in on everything the moment he had arrived at the castle. He strode into the room like he had every right to, standing tall despite his short stature.

Aurelius' entry changed the dynamics of the room. Audun always felt more at ease when his minister was present. The man was able to think fast on his feet and come up with plausible excuses and lies.

"Welcome, Aurelius. Glad to have you back. We are stuck in the dilemma of trying to figure out where the wedding of Korin and Adina should take place." Audun then proceeded to introduce him to the Carthinian dignitaries.

"Why naturally, it will have to take place in Carron, Your Highnesses," he replied in a smooth tone.

"Nonsense! Adina wants to be wed in her homeland, and that's that," retorted Tara.

"With all due respect, Your Highness, this would be of no issue under different circumstances. As a matter of fact, that *was* the Queen's original plan. However, her death has changed everything. Our customs forbid any royal member from participating in any ceremony, *especially* one as important as a wedding, outside the borders of Carron out of respect for the dead until the passage of one year," he lied with complete conviction.

Even Audun and Korin were astounded by Aurelius' skill at coming up with such plausible stories off the cuff. He was indeed infallibly cool under pressure. They chimed in their agreement. "That's very true."

Tara looked at them with arched brows, not believing this fabricated tale for a moment.

However, Adina's weeping face emerged from her tear-soaked hands, and she was overcome with sentiment for the dead Queen. "We *cannot* disrespect the dead. I'll wed in Carron," she replied.

Korin turned to her and embraced her, holding her tight. And Adina couldn't have been more pleased. Her tears vanished, and a radiating smile made an appearance on her face. Secure in Korin's arms, her heart throbbed in joy as if it wanted to escape her chest and dance. It made her proud to please him.

Tara, on the other hand, shot her a look of venom that would have reduced Adina to dust had the queen the power to do so.

Tara immediately intervened. "Adina, my dear…you've always wanted to be wed in Carthinia. You've talked about it since you were a child."

"I know, but we *cannot* disrespect their customs, especially when it has to do with the departed. It can bring bad luck and suffering. I'll sacrifice my wishes to honor their customs," she insisted like a lovesick fool.

Tara and Camden were both annoyed by their daughter.

Camden stepped in to see if he could convince her otherwise. "My dear child, how many times have you told me of your dreams to wed in Carthinia? It's been your desire," he pleaded.

"I *won't* disrespect the dead, father. You *have* to understand," she argued back.

Tara was not going to entertain this any longer and decided to put an end to it. "Fine!

We'll have the wedding one year from now in Carthinia. Problem solved!"

This left everyone speechless, including Aurelius.

Audun glared at him to come up with something to fight back, but Aurelius' mind drew a blank.

Adina pulled herself away from Korin and approached her mother.

"I'm in perfect agreement with being wed here. Why must you both draw it out for a year? A *year* is an eternity," she pleaded like a child.

"A year will go by so quickly you won't even notice it," Tara attempted to placate her when she actually wanted to strangle her instead.

"Father, don't do this to me," she pleaded tearfully, looking at Camden. He couldn't bear to see her in this condition. However, this time he could not give in and had to support Tara's decision.

"Your mother is right. A year will be gone in no time at all. Besides, we can have Korin visiting us as often as he wants to in the meanwhile," he consoled her.

"She's right. A year *is* a very long time. It's especially long when two people are in love. Isn't that true?" Aurelius sided with Adina.

"Yes, it is," she replied eagerly.

"We'll have this wedding in Carthinia in one year, and that's final. We too have our customs. So far, we have given in to yours, and now it's time you respected ours," Tara stated sharply.

"That's true," Camden reiterated in support.

Adina was mortified at her father's refusal to side with her. She felt betrayed and couldn't understand why this had become a point of contention. She burst out of the room in tears, and this prompted Korin to follow her out.

"She'll get over her lovesickness. Are we understood? One year from now, the wedding will be held in Carthinia," concluded Tara.

Her tone grated on Audun's nerves, and he would have liked nothing more than to crush her bones. He despised her. At the risk of not throwing suspicion on his own devious plans, he agreed begrudgingly. This changed everything. Nevertheless, it gave them time to devise a different strategy.

The visit eventually came to an end, and the visitors prepared to leave. The huge procession got ready for its long trek back to Carthinia. Adina was heartbroken and wept bitterly the entire time.

Korin pitied her and accompanied his betrothed to the gates of the city. He bid her farewell and walked away without looking back. But Adina's tear-soaked face remained turned around, staring at his back until the giant gates were closed shut.

THE WOLVES SHOT THROUGH the forest carrying their riders to safety: some wounded and others unscathed.

A few remaining marauders continued to give chase into the forest, but it wasn't long before the ever-alert guardians mauled them to death. Screams and sounds of cracking bones were heard as the mammoth beasts tore through them viciously.

Raidon and Eyvind didn't realize they were both bleeding from injuries until they reached the inner forest where the colossal trees were rooted. Eyvind had a deep cut on his right upper arm that kept dripping blood and sullying the snow-white fur of the wolf. Raidon had a serious knife wound to his thigh that was making him woozy. Yet the two men never complained and never stopped.

Upon reaching the inner forest, the beasts came to a halt, and the riders dismounted. Raidon was puzzled when he looked around the white barks of the trees.

Why are we stopping here? There's no sign of civilization anywhere. His spiraling thoughts stopped when the Bal-Sherans opened the invisible doors in the trees and disappeared through them.

He looked up at the giant trees, and all he could see was a canopy of smaller white trees. This confused his exhausted mind. Even in his imagination, he would have never expected an arboreal civilization.

He turned to look at Eyvind with rounded eyes, questions swirling within them. Eyvind lifted Raidon's arm and placed it across his own shoulders. "Come. Let me help you. There are steps here." He helped Raidon up the spiraling stairs that led them to the city in the clouds. Raidon was left astounded with each climb of the steps.

Taking in the sights, Raidon ascended the seemingly endless number of steps. *There has to be more than a hundred here.* His tired mind could think no further when, at the top, his eyes took in the city that was anchored on the treetops, as if they were living among the clouds. He had never expected such a city to exist in the forest, suspended in the air. It was the most beautiful place he had ever seen. He wondered if this was where the Imen lived in Carron.

The Bal-Sherans immediately rushed over to assist and help them. The healers were summoned in haste to tend to the injuries of all the men.

Eyvind was bothered by a pressing question as he lay in wait for the healers.

"Were you pursued by soldiers by any chance?" he asked Raidon, keeping his voice low.

"Yes," he replied with regret.

Eyvind became concerned and knew Aurelius would not rest until he found Roni, especially now that he was on their trail.

"You know he'll come after us. He won't cease until he captures us. And Roni," replied Eyvind in a somber tone.

Raidon was aware of this. They both looked around at the beautiful city and the Bal-Sherans. "We cannot let harm come to them," Eyvind stated.

"What do you suggest?" he asked.

Eyvind waited for a few moments as he pondered the question and tried to come up with a logical answer, but his mind drew a complete blank. "I'm not sure just yet," he responded.

They were both interrupted when Roni entered the chamber. Raidon was taken aback by how majestic she looked. She rushed to him and hugged him tightly in relief.

"You look fine enough to be a Queen," he stated with a smile.

"She will soon be crowned our Queen," replied Doru from the other side of the room with great enthusiasm.

"What?" asked Raidon in surprise.

"It's true. She's their Queen," affirmed Eyvind.

"How about that!" Raidon stated in astonishment. "This adventure gets better and better. Pardon my manners, Your Highness." Raidon was embarrassed by his impetuousness.

Roni took his hand and enveloped it in both of hers. "Your manners are perfect, Raidon. Thank you for risking your life for me. I'm so glad to see you alive and well. It's all that matters."

Her eyes shone with gratitude and relief to see both Eyvind and Raidon relatively unharmed. Seeing the sparkle on her face, Eyvind was mesmerized. He was unaware of the pain of his injury at the hands of the healer, who was busy wrapping his wound.

Hypnotized by Roni's beauty, he stared at her through exhausted eyes, and it wasn't much longer before he passed out.

Everyone else retired for the night.

Sometime later, Eyvind woke up and found himself staring up at the dark sky studded with a million twinkling stars through his window. A feeling of doom passed through him. He felt ill on the inside and knew it concerned his mother. He wanted to go back home to check on her but was aware certain death awaited him. However, he vowed he would not rest until he knew what happened to her and until justice was done.

The sick feeling continued to pummel his body in waves, making his gut clench and leaving him drained. Unable to rest, the whole night he lay shivering on the bed, with tears dripping down his face. There was a hollow feeling deep inside his core, where his instincts told him that his mother had passed. And he knew it was not a natural death. He silently made a promise to himself to investigate the whole incident, and if that was indeed so, he would avenge her death. But first, he needed to rest and focus on the next day. Roni and the other Bal-Sherans had to be protected against Aurelius, and Audun's army.

Eyvind was a man without a country and a commander without an army.

The next morning, Roni was to be formally introduced to the Bal-Sherans with the rituals of her coronation to commence the following day. It was a day full of events and festivities that involved several ceremonies to be performed at various sacred locations.

But before their commencement, Eyvind requested an audience with the Elders and

Roni. His request was granted with Raidon also in attendance. The Elders were baffled by this strange and urgent request in the middle of their busy schedule, but they couldn't refuse the Queen's orders. They assembled in the great hall where Eyvind and Raidon were already waiting for them.

Everyone took their respective seats with a throne being added for Roni.

"What's so pressing and urgent?" asked Shuzuko.

Eyvind stepped closer and addressed his concerns in a grave tone. "With all due respect, I apologize for taking your time but I...we need to bring something to your attention urgently."

They leaned back in their chairs, wondering what surprise the two Carronites had in store for them."Go on," urged Shuzuko.

"The soldiers from Carron followed Raidon to the mountain range and know where we've escaped to—"

He was interrupted by Kirio. "Th-they know about Bal-Shera?"

"No, even we didn't know about Bal-Shera. But the King's army will soon find out where we went." His voice carried a feeling of doom which made the Elders apprehensive.

"Maybe there was some truth in our rule to not let strangers into Bal-Shera," stated another Elder, shaking his head ruefully. "Now, they come hunting for their fugitives."

"It is not just us they seek," Eyvind clarified. His statement caused a stir among the assembly.

"What do you mean by that? Who else would they come after?" asked Kirio.

"Yes. Who else?" they asked.

"It's Queen Roni they seek the most," he replied.

"Roni? The Queen?" they remarked, wondering why she would be sought after. The chamber was in chaos, and the Elders became restless.

Eyvind didn't waste time and disclosed why Aurelius was after her.

"But she no longer possesses any powers. Do they not know that?" argued an Elder.

"The Imen are a myth in my land. Most don't even know of their existence, and those who do find out have only their imaginations to give fabricated details of what the Imen are capable of," replied Raidon.

"As far as they're concerned, she's capable of tremendous magical powers, and the proof is in her escape from the woodcutter's cabin," Eyvind added.

They listened intently with growing concern. At first, it was hard to believe, but then they accepted the warning. However, they still did not appear alarmed, and in fact, a few snickered at the mention of a possible attack.

"There's no need for alarm. Let them come! Many have tried in the past but have failed. They'll never find our city in the sky. Also, they cannot pass through the forest with the giant wolves to even reach us. With all the barriers that exist between the Talbot Range and Bal-Shera, there is hardly any hope of seeing a stranger make it this far," stated Shuzuko with confidence.

"*We* made it through," reminded Raidon.

"Only with *our* help. Do not forget that," reminded Nouri.

"You're correct. However, these men are determined," warned Raidon.

"And our environment is also determined to keep them out. Between the Demon wind, the underground marauders, the giant wolves, and the secret world aloft, they will never reach us," Kirio stated in their defense.

Eyvind and Raidon could not deny that. Her statement made it difficult to argue any further. They politely thanked them for their time and excused themselves. They sensed they stood no chance of convincing them otherwise. The Bal-Sherans had no concept of a relentless, vicious, and determined enemy who would do everything to reach them and then some.

Roni remained silent throughout the conversation since she was not qualified to speak on behalf of the Bal-Sherans until her official coronation.

The two men walked away, each lost in thought.

"Sire, do you think the safeguards the Bal-Sherans have will hold good in the future?" Raidon asked.

"I don't know. But I hope they will, for Roni's sake." Eyvind's answer had a thread of worry weaving through it.

"Can Aurelius penetrate all these hardships and reach here? We too found it nearly impossible to traverse," remarked Raidon.

Eyvind thought for a moment and then answered. "It's hard to say. It depends on how badly he wants to pursue her. So far, he has not succeeded in acquiring anything other than the woodcutter, and I have his Book of Spells."

"You do?" asked Raidon. "Where is it?

"I had it tucked in my tunic during the journey and have carried it this far. I planned on burning it the first chance I got," he replied. "At first, I was going to feed it to the Demon wind, but then I realized the pages might scatter all over and fall into evil hands. So, I made the decision to feed the book to the flames instead and be rid of it forever."

"Then we must do it the first chance we get," suggested Raidon.

They looked at one another, and both had the same idea. "There's no better time than now," they said in unison.

Eyvind touched a burning stick to the book, and the flame danced across the thick cover to reach its inside. The two Carronites stared as the pages charred and then reduced to curly bits of ash. A plume of smoke rose high into the sky like a dark serpent struggling upward until every last page was destroyed.

Then the sparks flew, and the cover caught the flames. The gold-gilded leather cover contorted and burned slowly, giving off a stench of burning flesh. The men remained planted on their spot until the twisted cover smoldered slowly and presented no threat to anyone anymore as it no longer held any secret spells. The entire book was eaten up by the fire in a few moments.

The following day, ceremonies extended throughout the waking hours. Roni was whisked from one event to the other in haste. Eyvind and Raidon managed to join the festivities. Both felt a sense of relief at having burned the dreaded Book of Spells. Now, Aurelius would never be able to get his hands on it.

Eyvind was polite and courteous to everyone who came to have a word with him, but Raidon sensed something was amiss with him, as his smile never reached his eyes. He was not quite himself.

At first, Raidon thought it had something to do with Michio, the son of Elder Kirio, who was seen accompanying Roni during the rituals. But then he was astute enough to realize it was something deeper than that. Eyvind's entire demeanor had worry and sadness embedded in it. Raidon didn't want to pry but felt he needed to.

"Sire? Something heavy is burdening you. What is it?" he asked politely.

Eyvind didn't know what to say or how to answer him because he didn't want to voice his fears of what he thought had occurred.

"Sire?" Raidon prodded again.

"I think it's my mother. I'm certain she's dead. And it's not by natural cause," Eyvind replied abruptly, his eyes filling with tears.

"If that's true, we'll avenge her death, Sire," Raidon vowed.

Eyvind nodded. "We'll need an army for that, and we don't have the resources at the moment. We're mere refugees for now."

"Then we'll return to Carron and begin to enlist dissidents and build our army to fight back to put order and justice in its proper place," replied Raidon, determination underscoring his words.

Eyvind smiled and nodded in agreement as he felt the first ember of hope at this. The idea was noble but dangerous. The duo moved on and spent the day watching Roni attend various functions and events and perform all the rituals with grace. She occasionally looked up as if searching for them, but the Elders diverted her attention by continually ushering her from one function to the next.

At the end of the evening, Eyvind found a quiet moment and retired to the highest vantage point in Bal-Shera and looked out in the direction of Carron. He wondered what nefarious schemes his brother and father were up to.

His concentration was interrupted by soft footsteps behind him. He turned abruptly, a little startled, and saw it was Roni. The air vibrated around her, and everything in him calmed. She was like a mythical beauty, a spell-binding apparition, and the only person who could take his mind off the thoughts that consumed him.

Seeing Eyvind's appearance, Roni immediately sensed something was not right with him. "Am I intruding?" she asked.

"No, not at all." Eyvind scrambled toward her and took her by the hand. He stood face to face with her and stared into her eyes. She wished she still had the gift to search so she could see the source of his pain.

"What is it?" she asked in concern for him.

He wanted to hide what ailed him because he didn't want to spoil her moment.

Roni insisted on knowing. "Tell me."

"It's nothing. I'm happy for you," he lied.

She knew he was lying and stepped back from him.

"Something's happened. I know it because I feel it. What is it?" she asked again.

Eyvind knew he needed to be honest with her and tell her. But he couldn't find the words.

"Something's happened to someone close to you—is that so?" she asked, reading his expression.

He nodded without saying anything. He was impressed by her perceptiveness.

"Who? Your mother?" she guessed.

He nodded.

Roni sensed his grief and embraced him.

He felt peace and comfort in her arms. They both felt a surge of emotions that dangerously flirted with passion, and neither wanted to let go.

However, Roni forced herself to pull away. She was the future Queen of Bal-Shera, and her duties were laid out for her. She could not veer from them even if she wanted to. A storm of confusion swept over her. She knew what her heart wanted and what was expected of her by her people.

She was uncertain of what was deemed acceptable or not. So, she painfully chose to assume her new responsibilities, setting aside her personal desires. She was already paying the ultimate price for her selfish deeds.

Had Eyvind been an Imen, things would have been different for them. She would not have to contend with the Elders about the issues of the strangers in their land, let alone the willingness to accept one as their King.

She had to take small steps and hope that within time the Bal-Sherans would learn to accept him as their own. Only then would she stand a chance to proceed further. For now, she chose to fight against her personal wishes and stay on the path of duty.

Eyvind too understood her struggle and accepted her actions. Dismayed by the circumstances that had unfolded before him, his desire to be with her also had become a struggle for him. Besides, he had to return home to avenge his mother's death and save the people of Carron from the schemes his father and brother were plotting. Also, he had to release his brethren to the afterlife before putting his own desires ahead.

With a sigh, he released her completely and walked away, taking his heavy heart with him.

The following morning as Roni was soon to be crowned the Queen of Bal-Shera, the entire city was in a flurry of excitement as everyone started gathering for the event. The massive assembly platform at the center of Bal-Shera, connected by many walkways, was the site of the coronation ceremony. The people's exhilaration was palpable and electrifying.

Eyvind and Raidon were given garments fit for royalty as they were to be honored in a special ceremony for safely delivering their Queen.

And then the moment they had all been waiting for finally arrived. Roni made her slow progression down the path led by the Elders and the High Priest to her awaiting throne. She stepped into the room, and all eyes were trained on her. The dress she wore flowed like liquid pearl, a cascade of ivory that shimmered softly with her every step. Its neckline accentuated her collarbones while following the delicate curve of her neck.

A whisper of vintage lace trailed down the bodice, ending in an ornate ivory tunic that hugged her waist, creating a regal silhouette with its heavy embroidery and studded with precious stones that sparkled like stars. As she glided across the assembly floor, reminiscent of her dance movements in Imen-Hera, her long train followed her, leaving a faint trail of beauty and poise in her wake. There was something enchanting about the moment. Her dark hair, swept in an elegant updo, was kept in place by a single ivory pearl clip that twinkled in the light.

Roni walked in measured steps, exuding confidence and grace, until she reached the throne, where she was guided to sit. The High Priest recited several texts with formality until it was time for the actual coronation.

A junior priest arrived, holding a navy-blue pillow with a silver border lace. Upon it sat the most beautiful crown ever made. A solid piece of crystal that was artfully carved into the shape of a crown with fine grooves cut into it and inlaid with gold. The inlay pattern resembled fine vines and scrolls.

A large blue stone exactly like the one in Roni's ring was set in the center of the crown while other precious stones were inset throughout the circlet. The crown was not just a piece of jewelry but an embodiment of everything Roni was and what she stood for.

The High Priest lifted the crown and rested it upon her head and announced her as their Queen. The crowd burst into loud thunderous cheer that echoed all around. Applause could be heard from one end of Bal-Shera to the other. And then it was time for Roni's first speech as the Queen of Bal-Sheri .

She arose from her throne and addressed her subjects.

"People of Bal-Shera, it gives me great pleasure to serve you as your Queen. I vow to carry out my duties with responsibility and justice. I will lead you and guide you through lit passages and steer you away from darkness. With your help and loyalty, we will move forward. With courage and strength, we will walk toward our next chapter."

Everyone listened intently as she spoke further, each word vibrating in their hearts.

"Together, we'll change and adapt to remain powerful, defend our land, and help all those who come to our aid. Bal-Shera will be the crown jewel, the city closest to the stars. We shall descend upon those who threaten us with fury.

"We will be gracious for the knowledge bestowed upon us by the Creator and use it to gain trust, friendship, respect, and authority when needed. As Bal-Sherans, we will be the guardians of truth, justice, civility, and above all, freedom. We are Bal-Sherans, and I am proud to serve as your Queen."

The crowd burst into a loud roar and applauded. They didn't completely comprehend her message regarding the offer of aid to outsiders. They only knew their solitary way of life, living in isolation from the rest of the world. Nevertheless, they had entrusted her with their safety and accepted whatever direction she would steer them in, simply because it was written in the Ancient Text.

Eyvind and Raidon were both surprised and impressed by her speech. It was nebulous and different from her real spirit, but diplomatic and quite in tune to what was expected of her as a Queen. They knew how she exactly was. Had it not been for her sense of adventure and the urge to explore a world outside her own, she would have never been here. She was a risk-taker and an adventurer by nature.

"Loyal subjects, I would not be standing before you had it not been for three brave men who risked their lives for me. One lost his life along the way, and the other two are here with us today. These men made great sacrifices when they chose to leave their lives behind and became fugitives for my sake. May I have the honor to present Raidon, the Imperial Knight of Carron."

Raidon was not expecting any of this. He rose humbly to accept the cheers and applauses.

"And now, may I present Eyvind, the Prince of Carron, who not only risked his life for me but surrendered his claim to the throne."

The crowd cheered loud and long until horns were sounded to restore order and silence.

Eyvind rose and acknowledged people's enthusiasm with respectful appreciation.

Roni smiled and bowed to both in deep gratitude.

"I'll forever be indebted to them. I cannot forget the loyalty and devotion these men have shown me as well as their fallen companion. To mark their valor, I announce they are now citizens of Bal-Shera."

The crowd expressed mixed acceptance.

The Carronites bowed to the crowd and then to Roni and the Elders.

The coronation ceremony concluded, and the trumpets blared loudly, followed by festive music. Roni was paraded through Bal-Shera to greet her subjects. She asked Eyvind and Raidon to accompany her.

Eyvind watched her assume the role of Queen effortlessly. It came naturally to her. Meanwhile, his mother's death loomed in his mind and continued to bother him. He found himself slightly disconnected from everything as his mind spiraled into thoughts of what would become of them.

Roni was now the Queen and he, a mere fugitive...with the status of a refugee. He knew he was drawn to her and she, to him. Yet, each had their responsibilities to attend to.

The day eventually concluded with an enormous feast, music, and dancing.

"I think you should ask her for a dance," suggested Raidon.

Eyvind looked at him as though he was insane.

"Go," Raidon prodded.

"We're in Bal-Shera. We're not aware of their customs. What if my asking offends them?" he retorted.

Michio was firmly by Roni's side, and it was apparent the Council had quietly chosen him as her suitor. This brought added pain to Eyvind, but he reminded himself that Roni had made no promises to him, and the choice of a suitor depended upon her and also upon Bal-Sheran customs.

"So what? It's just a dance, harmless. Go on."

Eyvind waited for a moment and then took his friend's advice and approached her.

Roni had hoped for this.

They danced for a while and at first, neither said anything. Their silence spoke volumes. They understood each other without uttering a single word.

Elder Kirio was annoyed by Eyvind's impetuousness in asking Roni to dance. She immediately approached Michio and chastised him and ordered him to dance with Roni for the remainder of the evening.

Michio proceeded to the dance floor and approached them. "May I have this dance?" he asked Roni politely. Michio was very handsome and just as kind, a wise soul who understood people far better than they were aware of.

Eyvind relinquished Roni's hand to him. He was aware of Kirio's motives and chose to excuse himself.

It was obvious that although they were proclaimed honorary citizens of Bal-Shera, they were still outsiders. Only Roni considered them as Bal-Sheran. He did not want to disrespect Roni or any of the others or make things awkward here. He thus chose to resume his position as a Carronite and keep himself separate.

The festivities came to a conclusion, and Roni again thanked them both. She reiterated they were now citizens of Bal-Shera and would be expected to make this their home. They were appreciative of her gesture, and for now, this city would *have* to be their temporary home.

Raidon followed a varlet who showed him to his quarters.

Eyvind offered to walk Roni to her royal chamber. They both walked slowly, savoring the time and the moments they had with one another. Each wanted to speak, but neither could find the right words to say anything.

When they reached her chamber, he took her hand in his and gently kissed it. "It's strange how life unfolds surprises. Some with good outcomes and others with despair."

She nodded her head in agreement, keeping her smile in place, but he could see the pain swimming in her eyes.

"I stand so close to you, Roni, yet we're separated by a giant rift of cultures and ways of life."

Roni tried to speak, but he continued, "I have no regrets for having done what I did in choosing my path. I would do it all over again if I could. The most painful thing of all is loving someone you cannot have. I'm not vying for pity or anything. But I've come to accept that we both have our destinies to follow and someday our paths may cross again...and who knows where fate will deliver us." There was a strong note of hope in his voice.

Roni listened to him carefully and held back her emotions with great difficulty. She wanted to say so much but restrained herself. She had to choose her words carefully. "No rift of culture or chasm of rituals can keep us separated. Fate is not what delivers us anywhere. Fate is what gives us the will to proceed forth to our destination despite the obstacles. *We* choose our paths and create our future. Upon a clean slate of tomorrow, we scribe our destinies and desires.

"So, my beloved Eyvind, it is of your choosing what you desire. I'm bound to a duty that is far greater than my own personal desires from which I cannot find a way to escape," she replied with tearful eyes.

Eyvind was overcome by her wisdom. He bowed before her and took her hand and pressed her fingers to his lips.

Roni fought back the emotions she had for him and maintained her composure with great difficulty.

Eyvind released her hand and stepped back to take a long look at her. She was magnificent, and he couldn't keep his eyes off her.

"Raidon and I are going to prepare to depart for Carron soon."

Roni was shocked and terrified. "Why? You'll be killed! Is that what you want? They're looking for you. Waiting down there," she protested.

"I must go. I have no other choice. Aside from you, there's nothing here for me. I have important duties calling out to me in Carron," he answered.

Roni's eyes filled with tears as fear welled in her heart. She could hardly believe what he was saying. Shaken up by the news, she believed she would never see him again once he departed Bal-Shera.

"I have to disinter my brethren and give him a proper funeral. I have to avenge my mother's death and fight for the good people of Carron to put order back into a corrupt nation. But the most important task is to try and lead Aurelius away from pursuing you. I need to find a way to throw him off your trail. That's where my destiny lies," he explained.

Roni found it hard to believe his resolve, yet she couldn't argue with him and accepted his decision. Although she was in disagreement with him, there wasn't much she could do or say to sway his mind.

Her biggest fear was losing Eyvind and never to see him again. The only thing she could do was offer him help. "If you must go, then I'll send a troop to help you reach your destination. I beg you to change your mind and consider your decision. I'm offering you a new home here," she replied somberly.

"You must understand. You're bound by your duties as the Queen to your people. But before I go, I have to make an admission to you, lest I regret it in the future."

Roni lifted her head, with a frown creasing her forehead, puzzled about what he had to say.

Eyvind stepped forward and stood before her and again took her hands in his. He looked into her pain-filled eyes and began, "Before I leave, I have something to say. I don't mean to make you feel awkward, but I feel it's necessary to let you know because if I fall into the hands of those who seek me, I may never live to tell you these words, and I will regret that until my last living moment. Roni, I love you. And I will always love you until the end of time."

Roni's eyes filled with tears as she stepped closer to him, released her hands from his, and embraced him tightly. She did not want to let go. Roni sobbed quietly with her head buried in his chest.

Eyvind held on to her, tears drenching his face, at a loss for words to help console her. He too was feeling all that she was.

She finally found the strength to pull herself away from him and pressed her finger against his lips to stop him from saying anything further.

"You mustn't say anything more. I'm not at liberty to say what or how much I feel. You must understand," she stated with great pain. Her face was tear-soaked, and she wished she could have told him how much she too loved him.

Eyvind understood her situation and sympathized with her because she no longer had the freedom to make her own decisions. Every decision she made from now on would have to be thought through carefully, taking the Bal-Sherans and their wishes into consideration.

He understood her situation far more because he too had done the same in Carron until the day he renounced the throne. He stepped back, took one last look at her, and departed to his chamber.

IT WASN'T LONG AFTER the Carthinians' departure that Korin, Audun, and Aurelius met in the King's study. The tension was high, and everyone was on edge. Their plans had been upturned by Eyvind earlier and now by Tara. It seemed they had grossly underestimated her.

Aurelius faced the wrath of both Korin and Audun for letting Eyvind and Raidon as well as Roni escape.

"What happened to them? How could you lose them!" growled Korin as he jabbed Aurelius in the chest with his finger.

"You'd never believe it if I told you—" Aurelius tried to explain but was sharply interrupted.

"Well, try me!" yelled Korin in his face.

"It was sorcery. They vanished, Sire. Right before my eyes."

"Right before your *blind* eyes, you mean!" snapped Korin.

"How can someone disappear before your very eyes?" asked Audun, getting exasperated by his minister's answers.

"I've brought the sorcerer with me," Aurelius placated them.

"Sorcerer?" asked Audun.

Korin was annoyed beyond his threshold of tolerance, and Aurelius was well aware of it. He was on thin ice with the young Prince and didn't want to push him any further because he was aware of Korin's vicious cruelty. He asked them to follow him to the dungeon, and they did so reluctantly.

Bomo was locked up in a cell, slumped in one corner. He looked miserable and not-so-menacing. This was not what they were expecting.

"There he is, the sorcerer himself," Aurelius proudly pointed, thinking that he had done them a favor.

They moved closer to have a good look at him but were not impressed.

"Him? He looks like a primitive beast," replied Audun.

"What sort of sorcery can this brute perform?" mocked Korin.

Bomo remained silent while anger brewed within him. He had no loyalty to any nation nor any man. Bomo was a rogue hermit who lived in the forest away from everyone.

His only obsession in life was the accumulation of gold, and now it was with Roni and her magical powers. But at this moment, he was sitting in a cold, dark dungeon far away from his hoard of gold with no means of getting back. He had to think of a way to get out.

"I *am* a sorcerer," he grumbled and got to his feet. The ogre was large in stature with a huge head and ungainly limbs and golden yellow eyes that were starting to simmer in anger.

Korin moved closer to the cell to get a better look at the creature and laughed at him. "If you're a sorcerer, then how come you haven't conjured a spell to break yourself out of this cell?"

Bomo could not answer him but became increasingly angry at the mocking. His muscles firmed and trembled in rage.

"Sire, he can turn people to stone. I saw it with my own eyes," defended Aurelius.

Audun looked at Aurelius with suspicion and asked, "You? You saw it with *your* own eyes?"

"Well, not exactly like that, but—"

"But what? You didn't see *anything*, did you?" Korin interrupted when he saw Aurelius getting flustered.

"Sire, he had turned an Imen into a stone and then brought the stone home to change her back, but realized he had the wrong stone. Someone found the real stone and used his potion to turn her back to a person while we were searching for the right one —"

"What are you talking about? What are these stones?" yelled out Audun, losing his patience on hearing Aurelius ramble.

"They're the stones in his head," ridiculed Korin.

"Please, Sire, this man *is* capable of conjuring spells. His mother was the *sorceress* of the forest. He had actually captured an Imen," Aurelius begged, wanting so desperately to be believed.

"The Imen are a myth!" shouted Korin. "And if you believe in them, you're the fool!"

"They do exist! My Roni *is* an Imen," Bomo yelled out.

"But, Sire, your own brother had an encounter with them and even showed us the injury he'd received during a boar hunt. Your Highness can even verify the scar. I'm not making this up," he pleaded.

"Yes, well, he did show us a scar, and we were led to believe he could capture one and bring her back. Now I'm starting to wonder if it had been a ploy to get away," replied Audun.

"But, Your Highness, how can you doubt their existence? It's a written fact they exist," continued Aurelius.

"Have *you* seen one?" asked Korin.

"No, Sire, but I would have seen one, had she not rendered herself invisible," he replied.

"Yes! *I* would've captured 'er, but she slipped away from me," added Bomo, his fury causing his body to become rigid.

Aurelius feared Bomo's strength and anger. He had witnessed his power and rage firsthand at his home. Without divulging it to Audun or Korin, he asked if they could resume the conversation back in the King's chambers.

"Are you afraid he might change you into a slithering snake, which you already are?" Korin taunted.

Aurelius detested the mockery but kept his mouth shut.

Audun refused to leave as the ogre had captured his interest. His primitive appearance was a novelty to the King who had never imagined that a being like him existed in his forest. Whether he was a sorcerer or not, it didn't matter at all. At least, not to him.

"Imen, you say?" Audun asked, pacing back and forth in front of Bomo's cell.

"Yes! Imen. Tell His Highness about them," Aurelius instructed.

"She's mine an' no one else's. You let 'er get away!" Bomo yelled as he charged forth and grabbed the bars on the cell. He couldn't believe he had lost Roni. He'd had her in his hands, and then she was gone. Recalling all the events that had happened before he was thrown into prison, his blood started to boil, and his golden yellow eyes glittered, burning with rage.

He pulled on the bars with each mounting wave of anger until they began to loosen.

All three of them jumped back, watching Bomo in horror.

Several soldiers and guards rushed in and positioned themselves to attack the ogre.

Audun and Aurelius backed up to the stairs that would lead them out of the dungeon.

"Chain him! I want him alive!" yelled out Aurelius in fear.

Korin grabbed a whip and snapped it against the bars, hoping to hit Bomo's hands, but he kept missing.

This enraged Bomo even more. He worked furiously to rip the bars out. He managed to loosen one free; however, the gap was not big enough for him to squeeze through. He worked on prying the next one.

The guards tried to stop him by lashing him with whips from all sides. With each crack of the braided thong on his flesh, his rage increased tenfold and became an inferno. The ogre yelled and grunted as he worked to wrench the bars out of the ground.

It wasn't until he managed to wrest at least three that Korin dropped the whip and grabbed a sword from a soldier to defend himself and ran toward the stairway.

"You lied to me! Liar! Liar!" ranted Bomo.

Aurelius scrambled backward in haste up the stairs.

The soldiers protected Audun and Korin and urged them to leave. They were horrified by the creature's strength and resilience to intense whipping. Speechless, the three hurried up the stairs to safety and returned to the study where Korin slammed the door shut behind him and locked it.

"What was that!" he yelled out.

"Sire, that's the sorcerer. I brought him here to help us get an advantage over the enemy. He can conjure potions to turn men into stone, and we can use that to our advantage. Don't you think?" stated Aurelius.

"But what evidence do you have that he's capable of doing so?" quizzed Audun.

"We returned to his abode and found wet footsteps leading out of the tub into which he had poured the potion," he explained.

"Imbecile! Anyone can step into a tub and walk out, leaving wet footsteps on the ground! Is that what you base your ridiculous claims on?" retorted Korin.

"*No*, Sire. There were no footprints of a woman walking into the house, aside from the wet ones leaving the house. There was another odd thing about them. Those prints were fresh, yet we didn't see anyone leave, even though we were all outside. We saw nothing. Also, they stole the horses from right under our nose. No one saw a thing," he explained emphatically.

"You've gone mad," Korin replied in annoyance. "You let Eyvind and Raidon get away with your stupidity, and to cover your incompetence, you have fabricated this fantastic lie using that…that…creature you happened to find in the forest."

"No. No, Sire, I'm not lying," he pleaded.

Korin had had enough of Aurelius and wanted to get on with the business of how they were going to carry out their plans.

However, Audun was interested in Aurelius' sorcerer. He was well aware of the Imen and their powers. "If this ogre is really a sorcerer, then he needs to show me his skills. I want to see him turn someone into a stone."

Aurelius calculated the success of his next few words and thought about a strategy. "Well... His Book of Spells was stolen by whoever released the Imen girl from the spell," he replied meekly.

"Then why did you bring him here? What good is he?" barked out Korin.

"I agree. What good is he?" joined Audun.

"He can recall the spell by heart," replied Aurelius.

"You know this for sure, or are you just guessing? You *are* insane, Aurelius!" bellowed Korin.

"Sire, he's worth a chance. He also claims he knows how to trap an Imen. That in itself is valuable because they can give us anything we want," he replied.

"Do you know the consequence of asking something from an Imen as opposed to receiving something unsolicited?" asked Audun.

"Yes, I do, Sire. I've weighed it out. A small sacrifice is worth making for a much bigger gain. Don't you agree?" he stated with confidence.

"And just how's he going to trap an Imen? With *his* 'good looks,' I suppose?" sneered Korin in a sarcastic tone, his derision for Bomo and Aurelius apparent on his face.

"He says he can get them to appear. I believe him," Aurelius replied as if he were Bomo's minister and not Audun's.

"Then let's have him show us," agreed Audun.

"Very well, Your Highness. I'll arrange for it immediately. But first, he has to be restrained," replied Aurelius in satisfaction.

Aurelius hurried back down to the dungeon and found absolute chaos raging there.

Several soldiers lay on the floor, limp and barely alive. A loud ruckus was heard down the narrow dark hallways.

Aurelius knew the woodcutter was not one to capitulate. He would fight to the bitter end. The minister plastered himself against the dark stone walls and slid along as carefully as he could, hoping not to get caught by the ruffian. He wondered where the brute was.

Aurelius' heart pounded hard and fast against his rib cage like a wild animal trying to break free. He felt death close by. Loud yells and screams were heard. A small troop of soldiers hurried past. He grabbed one of them by the arm. "What's going on?"

"The brute. He's escaped, Sire," replied the frightened soldier.

"What do you mean—escaped? How could you let him get away?" he asked in anger.

"He broke through and attacked everyone," the guard replied.

"Where's he now?" Aurelius asked in fear.

"He got out, Sire."

"Out? Where?" Aurelius asked in horror.

"Don't know. In the streets somewhere."

Aurelius straightened his body and firmed his shoulders and hurried down the hall after the soldier until he came to the courtyard where a huge commotion had taken place.

Bomo, after escaping from the dungeon in a fit of rage, had bowled down several soldiers and bent their swords as if they were made of putty. He had taken off on a horse and was last seen heading toward the city gates.

Most refused to stop him after witnessing the display of brute strength for which no one was a match. Others had no idea what was going on. Only a few tried to stop him in time but to no avail.

"Sound the alarm!" yelled out Aurelius as he ran up to the turret.

By the time the alarm was sounded, Bomo was only yards away from the gate.

The soldiers scrambled to close the heavy doors, but Bomo pushed the horse harder and managed to beat the closing gap. He squeezed through an opening barely wide enough to let the horse pass. Bomo heard the gates slam shut behind him as he briefly glanced back to check on his pursuers.

The ogre pushed the horse harder as the fire of his anger raged through his veins. His primitive mind had not considered the consequences of his actions. He was only concerned with the gold hoard hidden in his house. He had to get to it and see that it was still there and safe.

The ogre cut through the forest at great speed. He had never ridden on horseback before and was surprised he could control the animal with such ease. He was used to his ox and cart. He decided he would keep this horse for himself.

Before he knew it, he had arrived at his abode. Dismounting, he ran into his disturbed lair. The entire place looked as if it had been ransacked, with upturned furniture, broken pots, and ripped books. Exactly as he had left it. He pushed his way through until he reached his study. Everything was thrown about, and broken furniture lay scattered.

With a swift sweep of his gigantic arm, he cleared the floor clean where his hoard was concealed. He scrambled to lift the stones off the floor to reveal the golden chest that lay hidden underneath.

Bomo reached down and pulled it out in great relief. He opened it with feverish haste, causing the contents to fall out.

The ogre frantically watched his precious gold pieces scatter everywhere. He tried to put the box down, but there was no place to set it amongst the clutter. The whole room was a disaster. Coins fell between piles of ripped books and broken bits of furniture.

He began collecting his fallen gold pieces one by one while fervently cursing out loud without pausing, personifying the enraged madman that he was.

Immediately after sounding the alarm, Aurelius sent out a troop of soldiers to capture the ogre. They followed his trail into the forest and eventually arrived at his lair, where they saw the getaway horse outside.

Some soldiers surrounded the visible part of the exterior, and many of them carefully made their way in. Bomo's loud curses could be heard from deep within.

They entered room after room with their swords drawn and their steps muffled. Everyone was scared of what they would find, beads of sweat dripped from their foreheads. They knew what he had done to their comrades back in the dungeon.

The ruckus and curses became louder with each step.

They eventually reached the study where they saw the creature rummaging around, chucking books and various bits of broken furniture across the cluttered room and picking up pieces of gold from the floor. He looked diabolically menacing.

They were afraid at first, but then the leader of the troop ordered them to attack. With one leap forward, they entered the room and took Bomo by surprise. They fearfully approached him, not knowing what to expect next.

They made the mistake of entering his lair at the most sacred moment when the ogre was inspecting and handling his hoard. It was akin to entering a lion's cage at feast time.

They startled him as he was busily picking up his gold pieces from nooks and crevasses, where they had fallen, with his back to the door. The gold pieces lay about the room like sparkling dots as the ogre intensely searched for each precious coin.

The moment his eyes saw the soldiers, he seethed in rage and charged wildly at them with whatever he found lying about.

Bodies of soldiers were flung high and low as loud cries of pain rang out. Several more soldiers rushed in, only to discover the mayhem that Bomo was and cried out, "Stop!"

But there was no response from the fuming ogre. He continued to thrust missiles of busted furniture at them.

They swerved and ducked, some had to twist and sidestep to avoid being pelted.

Then came the order to fire at will from their leader. The soldiers then sheathed their swords and nocked the arrows to their bows, took aim, and with a final prayer, they released a volley of arrows in his direction.

The shafts flew toward him all at once, a couple of them found their mark. As a maneuver of survival, Bomo turned and kept his back to them. The arrows now had a bigger area to pierce. At first, the creature seemed unaffected and stood tall, but the barrage didn't slow down as the soldiers, fearing for their lives, kept at it. Time stood still for them even as seconds ticked away.

Finally, Bomo staggered and collapsed in a heap on the ground.

The soldiers stood motionless as they stared at the massive mound and the glimmering loot that lay scattered in the dimly lit, upturned room, with arrows tautly stretched on their bowstrings, at the ready.

AND HERE, THE *PURSUIT* continued for power, lust, and gold, while others were *Scattered* in unknown surroundings.

To be continued…

Volume Four, Imen of Atlantis: Scattered